Joseph Lewis French

Detective Stories

Joseph Lewis French

Detective Stories

ISBN/EAN: 9783955630386

Auflage: 1

Erscheinungsjahr: 2013

Erscheinungsort: Bremen, Deutschland

@ Leseklassiker in Access Verlag GmbH, Fahrenheitstr. 1, 28359 Bremen. Alle Rechte beim Verlag und bei den jeweiligen Lizenzgebern.

Leseklassiker

Foreword

The honour of founding the modern detective story belongs to an American writer. Such tales as "The Purloined Letter" and "The Murders in the Rue Morgue" still stand unrivalled.

We in America no more than the world of letters at large, did not readily realize what Poe had done when he created Auguste Dupin — the prototype of Sherlock Holmes *et genus omnes*, up to the present hour. On Poe's work is built the whole school of French detective story writers. Conan Doyle derived his inspiration from them in turn, and our American writers of to-day are helped from both French and English sources. It is rare enough to find the detective in fiction even to-day, however, who is not lacking in one supreme quality, — scientific imagination. Auguste Dupin had it. Dickens, had he lived a short time longer, might have turned his genius in this direction. The last thing he wrote was the "Mystery of Edwin Drood," the mystery of which is still unravelled. I have heard the opinion expressed by an eminent living writer that had Dickens' life been prolonged he would probably have become the greatest master of the detective story, except Poe.

The detective story heretofore has been based upon one of two methods: analysis or deduction. The former was Poe's, to take the typical example; the latter is Conan Doyle's. Of late the discoveries of science have been brought into play in this field of fiction with notable results. The most prominent of such innovators, indeed the first one, is Arthur Reeve, an American writer, whose "Black Hand" will be found in this collection; which has endeavoured within its limited space to cover the field from the start — the detective story — wholly the outgrowth of the more highly developed police methods which have sprung into being within little more than half a century, being only so old.

Joseph Lewis French.

Contents

I. The Purloined Letter — Edgar Allan Poe	1
II. The Black Hand — Arthur B. Reeve	27
III. The Bitter Bit — Wilkie Collins	56
IV. Missing: Page Thirteen — Anna Katherine Green	95
V. A Scandal in Bohemia — A. Conan Doyle	144
VI. The Rope of Fear — Mary E. and Thomas W. Hanshew	177
VII. The Safety Match — Anton Chekhov	203
VIII. Some Scotland Yard Stories — Sir Robert Anderson	232

I. The Purloined Letter — Edgar Allan Poe

Nil sapientiæ odiosius acumine nimio. — Seneca.

At Paris, just after dark one gusty evening in the autumn of 18 —, I was enjoying the twofold luxury of meditation and meerschaum, in company with my friend, C. Auguste Dupin, in his little back library, or book-closet, *au troisième*, No. 33 Rue Dunôt, Faubourg St. Germain. For one hour at least we had maintained a profound silence; while each, to any casual observer, might have seemed intently and exclusively occupied with the curling eddies of smoke that oppressed the atmosphere of the chamber. For myself, however, I was mentally discussing certain topics which had formed matter for conversation between us at an earlier period of the evening; I mean the affair of the Rue Morgue and the mystery attending the murder of Marie Roget. I looked upon it, therefore, as something of a coincidence, when the door of our apartment was thrown open and admitted our old acquaintance, Monsieur G—, the Prefect of the Parisian police.

We gave him a hearty welcome; for there was nearly half as much of the entertaining as of the contemptible about the man, and we had not seen him for several years. We had been sitting in the dark, and Dupin now arose for the purpose of lighting a lamp, but sat down again, without doing so, upon G— 's saying that he had called to consult us, or rather to ask the opinion of my friend, about some official business which had occasioned a great deal of trouble.

"If it is any point requiring reflection," observed Dupin, as he forbore to enkindle the wick, "we shall examine it to better purpose in the dark."

"That is another of your odd notions," said the Prefect, who had the fashion of calling everything "odd" that was beyond his comprehension, and thus lived amid an absolute legion of "oddities."

"Very true," said Dupin, as he supplied his visitor with a pipe and rolled toward him a comfortable chair.

"And what is the difficulty now?" I asked. "Nothing more in the assassination way, I hope?"

"Oh, no; nothing of that nature. The fact is, the business is very simple indeed, and I make no doubt that we can manage it sufficiently well ourselves; but then I thought Dupin would like to hear the details of it, because it is so excessively odd."

"Simple and odd?" said Dupin.

"Why, yes; and not exactly that either. The fact is, we have all been a good deal puzzled because the affair is so simple, and yet baffles us altogether."

"Perhaps it is the very simplicity of the thing which puts you at fault," said my friend.

"What nonsense you do talk!" replied the Prefect, laughing heartily.

"Perhaps the mystery is a little too plain," said Dupin.

"Oh, good heavens! who ever heard of such an idea?"

"A little too self-evident."

"Ha! ha! ha! — ha! ha! ha! — ho! ho! ho!" roared our visitor, profoundly amused. "Oh, Dupin, you will be the death of me yet!"

"And what, after all, is the matter on hand?" I asked.

"Why, I will tell you," replied the Prefect, as he gave a long, steady, and contemplative puff and settled himself in his chair, — "I will tell you in a few words; but, before I begin, let me caution you that this is an affair demanding the greatest secrecy, and that I should most probably lose the position I now hold were it known that I confided it to anyone."

"Proceed," said I.

"Or not," said Dupin.

"Well, then; I have received personal information, from a very high quarter, that a certain document of the last importance has been purloined from the royal apartments. The individual who purloined it is known — this beyond a doubt; he was seen to take it. It is known, also, that it still remains in his possession."

"How is this known?" asked Dupin.

"It is clearly inferred," replied the Prefect, "from the nature of the document and from the non-appearance of certain results which would at once arise from its passing out of the robber's possession, that is to say, from his employing it as he must design in the end to employ it."

"Be a little more explicit," I said.

"Well, I may venture so far as to say that the paper gives its holder a certain power in a certain quarter where such power is immensely valuable." The Prefect was fond of the cant of diplomacy.

"Still I do not quite understand," said Dupin.

"No? Well; the disclosure of the document to a third person, who shall be nameless, would bring in question the honour of a personage of most exalted station; and this fact gives the holder of the document an ascendency over the illustrious personage whose honour and peace are so jeopardized."

"But this ascendency," I interposed, "would depend upon the robber's knowledge of the loser's knowledge of the robber. Who would dare — "

"The thief," said G—, "is the Minister D—, who dares all things, those unbecoming as well as those becoming a man. The method of the theft was not less ingenious than bold. The document in question, — a letter, to be frank, — had been received by the personage robbed while alone in the royal boudoir. During its perusal she was suddenly interrupted by the entrance of the other exalted personage from whom especially it was her wish to conceal it. After a hurried and vain endeavour to thrust it in a drawer, she was forced to place it, open as it was, upon a table. The address, however, was uppermost, and, the contents thus unexposed, the letter escaped notice. At this juncture enters the Minister D—. His lynx eye immediately perceives the paper, recognizes the handwriting of the address, observes the confusion of the personage addressed, and fathoms her secret. After some business transactions, hurried through in his ordinary manner, he produces a letter somewhat similar to the one in question, opens it, pretends to read it, and then places it in close juxtaposition to the other. Again he converses for some fifteen minutes upon the public affairs. At length, in taking leave, he takes also from the table the letter to which he had no claim. Its rightful owner saw, but, of course, dared not call attention to the act, in the presence of the third personage, who stood at her elbow. The Minister decamped, leaving his own letter, one of no importance, upon the table."

"Here, then," said Dupin to me, "you have precisely what you demand to make the ascendency complete, the robber's knowledge of the loser's knowledge of the robber."

"Yes," replied the Prefect; "and the power thus attained has, for some months past, been wielded, for political purposes, to a very dangerous extent. The personage robbed is more thoroughly convinced every day of the necessity of reclaiming her letter. But this, of course, cannot be done openly. In fine, driven to despair, she has committed the matter to me."

"Than whom," said Dupin, amid a perfect whirlwind of smoke, "no more sagacious agent could, I suppose, be desired or even imagined."

"You flatter me," replied the Prefect; "but it is possible that some such opinion may have been entertained."

"It is clear," said I, "as you observe, that the letter is still in the possession of the Minister; since it is this possession, and not any employment of the letter, which bestows the power. With the employment the power departs."

"True," said G—; "and upon this conviction I proceeded. My first care was to make thorough search of the Minister's hotel; and here my chief embarrassment lay in the necessity of searching without his knowledge. Beyond all things, I have been warned of the danger which would result from giving him reason to suspect our design."

"But," said I, "you are quite *au fait* in these investigations. The Parisian police have done this thing often before."

"Oh, yes; and for this reason I did not despair. The habits of the Minister gave me, too, a great advantage. He is frequently absent from home all night. His servants are by no means numerous. They sleep at a distance from their master's apartment, and, being chiefly Neapolitans, are readily made drunk. I have keys, as you know, with which I can open any chamber or cabinet in Paris. For three months a night has not passed, during the greater part of which I have not been engaged, personally, in ransacking the D— Hotel. My honour is interested, and, to mention a great secret, the reward is enormous. So I did not abandon the search until I had become fully satisfied that the thief is a more astute man than myself. I fancy that I have investigated every nook and corner of the premises in which it is possible that the paper can be concealed."

"But is it not possible," I suggested, "that although the letter may be in possession of the Minister, as it unquestionably is, he may have concealed it elsewhere than upon his own premises?"

"This is barely possible," said Dupin. "The present peculiar condition of affairs at court, and especially of those intrigues in which D— is known to be involved, would render the instant availability of the document, its susceptibility of being produced at a moment's notice, a point of nearly equal importance with its possession."

"Its susceptibility of being produced?" said I.

"That is to say, of being destroyed," said Dupin.

"True," I observed; "the paper is clearly, then,

upon the premises. As for its being upon the person of the minister, we may consider that as out of the question."

"Entirely," said the Prefect. "He has been twice waylaid, as if by footpads, and his person rigidly searched under my own inspection."

"You might have spared yourself this trouble," said Dupin. "D—, I presume, is not altogether a fool, and, if not, must have anticipated these waylayings, as a matter of course."

"Not altogether a fool," said G—, "but then he is a poet, which I take to be only one remove from a fool."

"True," said Dupin, after a long and thoughtful whiff from his meerschaum, "although I have been guilty of certain doggerel myself."

"Suppose you detail," said I, "the particulars of your search."

"Why, the fact is, we took our time, and we searched everywhere. I have had long experience in these affairs. I took the entire building, room by room; devoting the nights of a whole week to each. We examined, first, the furniture of each apartment. We opened every possible drawer; and I presume you know that, to a properly trained police-agent, such a thing as a 'secret' drawer is impossible. Any man is a dolt who permits a 'secret' drawer to escape him in a search of this kind. The thing is so plain. There is a certain amount of bulk, of space, to be accounted for in every cabinet. Then we have accurate rules. The fiftieth part of a line could not escape us. After the cabinets we took the chairs. The cushions we probed with the fine long needles you have seen me employ. From the tables we removed the tops."

"Why so?"

"Sometimes the top of a table or other similarly arranged piece of furniture is removed by the person wishing to conceal an article; then the leg is excavated, the article deposited within the cavity, and the top replaced. The bottoms and tops of bedposts are employed in the same way."

"But could not the cavity be detected by sounding?" I asked.

"By no means, if, when the article is deposited, a sufficient wadding of cotton be placed around it. Besides, in our case, we were obliged to proceed without noise."

"But you could not have removed, you could not have taken to pieces all articles of furniture in which it would have been possible to make a deposit in the manner you mention. A letter may be compressed into a thin spiral roll, not differing much in shape or bulk from a large knitting-needle, and in this form it might be inserted into the rung of a chair, for example. You did not take to pieces all the chairs?"

"Certainly not, but we did better: we examined the rungs of every chair in the hotel, and, indeed, the jointings of every description of furniture, by the aid of a most powerful microscope. Had there been any traces of recent disturbance we should not have failed to detect it instantly. A single grain of gimlet-dust, for example, would have been as obvious as an apple. Any disorder in the gluing, any unusual gaping in the joints, would have sufficed to insure detection."

"I presume you looked to the mirrors, between the boards and the plates, and you probed the beds and the bedclothes, as well as the curtains and carpets."

"That of course; and when we had absolutely completed every particle of the furniture in this way, then we examined the house itself. We divided its entire surface into compartments, which we numbered, so that none might be missed; then we scrutinized each individual square inch throughout the premises, including the two houses immediately adjoining, with the microscope, as before."

"The two houses adjoining!" I exclaimed; "you must have had a great deal of trouble."

"We had; but the reward offered is prodigious."

"You include the grounds about the houses?"

"All the grounds are paved with brick. They gave us comparatively little trouble. We examined the moss between the bricks and found it undisturbed."

"You looked among D— 's papers, of course, and into the books of the library?"

"Certainly; we opened every package and parcel; we not only opened every book, but we turned over every leaf in each volume, not contenting ourselves with a mere shake, according to the fashion of some of our police officers. We also measured the thickness of every book-cover with the most accurate measurement, and applied to each the most jealous scrutiny of the microscope. Had any of the bindings been recently meddled with, it would have been utterly impossible that the fact should have escaped observation. Some five or six volumes, just from the hands of the binder, we carefully probed, longitudinally, with the needles."

"You explored the floors beneath the carpets?"

"Beyond doubt. We removed every carpet and examined the boards with the microscope."

"And the paper on the walls?"

"Yes."

"You looked into the cellars?"

"We did."

"Then," I said, "you have been making a miscalculation, and the letter is not upon the premises, as you suppose."

"I fear you are right there," said the Prefect. "And now, Dupin, what would you advise me to do?"

"To make a thorough research of the premises."

"That is absolutely needless," replied G—. "I am not more sure that I breathe than I am that the letter is not at the hotel."

"I have no better advice to give you," said Dupin. "You have, of course, an accurate description of the letter?"

"Oh, yes!" and here the Prefect, producing a memorandum-book, proceeded to read aloud a minute account of the internal, and especially of the external, appearance of the missing document. Soon after finishing the perusal of this description he took his departure, more entirely depressed in spirits than I had ever known the good gentleman before.

In about a month afterward he paid us another

visit, and found us occupied very nearly as before. He took a pipe and a chair and entered into some ordinary conversation. At length I said:

"Well, but, G—, what of the purloined letter? I presume you have at last made up your mind that there is no such thing as overreaching the Minister?"

"Confound him! say I — yes; I made the re-examination, however, as Dupin suggested, but it was all labour lost, as I knew it would be."

"How much was the reward offered, did you say?" asked Dupin.

"Why, a very great deal, a very liberal reward; I don't like to say how much, precisely; but one thing I will say, — that I wouldn't mind giving my individual check for fifty thousand francs to anyone who could obtain me that letter. The fact is, it is becoming of more and more importance every day; and the reward has been lately doubled. If it were trebled, however, I could do no more than I have done."

"Why, yes," said Dupin, drawlingly, between the whiffs of his meerschaum, "I really — think, G—, you have not exerted yourself — to the utmost in this matter. You might — do a little more, I think, eh?"

"How? in what way?"

"Why — puff, puff — you might — puff, puff — employ counsel in the matter, eh? — puff, puff, puff. Do you remember the story they tell of Abernethy?"

"No; hang Abernethy!"

"To be sure! hang him and welcome. But, once

upon a time, a certain rich miser conceived the design of sponging upon this Abernethy for a medical opinion. Getting up, for this purpose, an ordinary conversation in a private company, he insinuated his case to the physician as that of an imaginary individual.

"'We will suppose,' said the miser, 'that his symptoms are such and such; now, Doctor, what would you have directed him to take?'

"'Take!' said Abernethy, 'why, take advice, to be sure.'"

"But," said the Prefect, a little discomposed, "I am perfectly willing to take advice and to pay for it. I would really give fifty thousand francs to anyone who would aid me in the matter."

"In that case," replied Dupin, opening a drawer and producing a checkbook, "you may as well fill me up a check for the amount mentioned. When you have signed it I will hand you the letter."

I was astounded. The Prefect appeared absolutely thunderstricken. For some minutes he remained speechless and motionless, looking incredulously at my friend with open mouth, and eyes that seemed starting from their sockets; then, apparently recovering himself in some measure, he seized a pen, and after several pauses and vacant stares finally filled up and signed a check for fifty thousand francs and handed it across the table to Dupin. The latter examined it carefully and deposited it in his pocketbook; then, unlocking an escritoire, took thence a letter and gave it to the Prefect. This functionary grasped it in a perfect agony of joy, opened it with a trembling hand, cast a rapid glance at its contents, and then, scrambling and struggling to the door, rushed at length unceremoniously from the room and from the house without having uttered a syllable since Dupin had requested him to fill up the check.

When he had gone, my friend entered into some explanations.

"The Parisian police," he said, "are exceedingly able in their way. They are persevering, ingenious, cunning, and thoroughly versed in the knowledge which their duties seem chiefly to demand. Thus, when G— detailed to us his mode of searching the premises at the Hotel D—, I felt entire confidence in his having made a satisfactory investigation, so far as his labours extended."

"'So far as his labours extended'?" said I.

"Yes," said Dupin. "The measures adopted were not only the best of their kind, but carried out to absolute perfection. Had the letter been deposited within the range of their search, these fellows would, beyond a question, have found it."

I merely laughed, but he seemed quite serious in all that he said.

"The measures, then," he continued, "were good in their kind and well executed; their defect lay in their being inapplicable to the case and to the man. A certain set of highly ingenious resources are, with the Prefect, a sort of Procrustean bed, to which he forcibly adapts his designs. But he perpetually errs by being too deep or too shallow for the matter in hand; and many a schoolboy is a better reasoner than he. I knew one about eight years of age, whose success at guessing in the game of 'even and odd' attracted universal admiration. This game is simple, and is played with marbles. One player holds in his hand a number of these toys and demands of another whether that number is even or odd. If the guess is right, the guesser wins one; if wrong, he loses one. The boy to whom I allude won all the marbles of the school. Of course he had some principle of guessing; and this lay in mere observation and admeasurement of the astuteness of his opponents. For example, an arrant simpleton is his opponent, and, holding up his closed hand, asks, 'Are they even or odd?' Our schoolboy replies, 'Odd,' and loses; but upon the second trial he wins, for he then says to himself: 'The simpleton had them even upon the first trial, and his amount of cunning is just sufficient to make him have them odd upon the second; I will therefore guess odd;' he guesses odd and wins. Now, with a simpleton a degree above the first, he would have reasoned thus: 'This fellow finds that in the first instance I guessed odd, and in the second he will propose to himself, upon the first impulse, a simple variation from even to odd, as did the first simpleton; but then a second thought will suggest that this is too simple a variation, and finally he will decide upon putting it even as before. I will therefore guess even;' — he guesses even and wins. Now this mode of reasoning in the schoolboy, whom his fellows termed 'lucky,' — what, in its last analysis, is it?"

"It is merely," I said, "an identification of the reasoner's intellect with that of his opponent."

"It is," said Dupin; "and upon inquiring of the boy by what means he effected the thorough identification in which his success consisted, I received answer as follows: 'When I wish to find out how wise, or how stupid, or how good, or how wicked is anyone, or what are his thoughts at the moment, I fashion the expression of my face, as accurately as possible, in accordance with the expression of his and then wait to see what thoughts or sentiments arise in my mind or heart, as if to match or correspond with the expression.' This response of the schoolboy lies at the bottom of all the spurious profundity which has been attributed to Rochefoucauld, to La Bruyère, to Machiavelli, and to Campanella."

"And the identification," I said, "of the reasoner's intellect with that of his opponent depends, if I understand you aright, upon the accuracy with which the opponent's intellect is admeasured."

"For its practical value it depends upon this," replied Dupin; "and the Prefect and his cohort fail so frequently, first, by default of this identification, and, secondly, by ill-admeasurement, or rather through non-admeasurement, of the intellect with which they are engaged. They consider only their own ideas of ingenuity; and, in searching for anything hidden, advert only to the modes in which they would have hidden it. They are right in this much, that their own ingenuity is a faithful representative of that of the mass; but when the cunning of the individual felon is diverse in character from their own the felon foils them, of course. This always happens when it is above their own, and very usually when it is below. They have no variation of principle in their investigations; at best, when urged by some unusual emergency, by some extraordinary reward, they extend or exaggerate their old modes of practice without touching their principles. What, for example, in this case of D—, has been done to vary the principle of action? What is all this boring, and probing, and sounding, and scrutinizing with the microscope, and dividing the surface of the building into registered square inches; what is it all but an exaggeration of the application of the one principle or set of principles of search, which are based upon the one set of notions regarding human ingenuity, to which the Prefect, in the long routine of his duty, has been accustomed? Do you not see he has taken it for granted that all men proceed to conceal a letter, not exactly in a gimlet-hole bored in a chair-leg, but, at least, in some out-of-the-way hole or corner suggested by the same tenor of thought which would urge a man to secrete a letter in a gimlet-hole bored in a chair-leg? And do you not see, also, that such *recherchés* nooks for concealment are adapted only for ordinary occasions, and would be adopted only by ordinary intellects; for, in all cases of concealment, a disposal of the article concealed, a disposal of it in this *rechercé* manner, is, in the very first instance, presumable and presumed; and thus its discovery depends, not at all upon the acumen, but altogether upon the mere care, patience, and determination of the seekers; and where the case is of importance, or, what amounts to the same thing in the policial eyes, when the reward is of magnitude, the qualities in question have never been known to fail. You will now understand what I meant in suggesting that, had the purloined letter been hidden anywhere within the limits of the Prefect's examination, — in other words, had the principle of its concealment been comprehended within the principles of the Prefect, — its discovery would have been a matter altogether beyond question. This functionary, however, has been thoroughly mystified; and the remote source of his defeat lies in the supposition that the Minister is a fool, because he has acquired renown as a poet. All fools are poets; this the Prefect feels; and he is merely guilty of a *non distributio medii* in thence inferring that all poets are fools."

"But is this really the poet?" I asked. "There are two brothers, I know; and both have attained reputation in letters. The Minister, I believe, has written learnedly on the Differential Calculus. He is a mathematician and no poet."

"You are mistaken; I know him well; he is both. As poet and mathematician, he would reason well; as mere mathematician, he could not have reasoned at all, and thus would have been at the mercy of the Prefect."

"You surprise me," I said, "by these opinions, which have been contradicted by the voice of the world. You do not mean to set at naught the well-digested idea of centuries? The mathematical reason has long been regarded as the reason *par excellence*."

"'Il y a à parier,'" replied Dupin, quoting from Chamfort, "'que toute idée publique, toute convention reçue, est une sottise, car elle a convenue au plus grand nombre.' The mathematicians, I grant you, have done their best to promulgate the popular error to which you allude, and which is none the less an error for its promulgation as truth. With an art worthy a better cause, for example, they have insinuated the term 'analysis' into application to algebra. The French are the originators of this particular deception; but if a term is of any importance, if words derive any value from applicability, then 'analysis' conveys 'algebra' about as much as, in Latin, '*ambitus*' implies 'ambition,' '*religio*' 'religion,' or '*homines honesti*' a set of honourable men."

"You have a quarrel on hand, I see," said I, "with some of the algebraists of Paris; but proceed."

"I dispute the availability, and thus the value of that reason which is cultivated in any especial form other than the abstractly logical. I dispute, in particular, the reason educed by mathematical study. The mathematics are the science of form and quantity; mathematical reasoning is merely logic applied to observation upon form and quantity. The great error lies in supposing that even the truths of what is called pure algebra are abstract or general truths. And this error is so egregious that I am confounded at the universality with which it has been received. Mathematical axioms are not axioms of general truth. What is true of relation, of form and quantity, is often grossly false in regard to morals, for example. In this latter science it is very usually untrue that the aggregated parts are equal to the whole. In chemistry, also, the axiom fails. In the consideration of motive it fails; for two motives, each of a given value, have not, necessarily, a value, when united, equal to the sum of their values apart. There are numerous other mathematical truths which are only truths within the limits of relation. But the mathematician argues from his finite truths, through habit, as if they were of an absolutely general applicability, as the world indeed imagines them to be. Bryant, in his very learned *Mythology*, mentions an analogous source of error when he says that 'although the pagan fables are not believed, yet we forget ourselves continually and make inferences from them as existing realities.' With the algebraists, however, who are pagans themselves, the 'pagan fables' are believed, and the inferences are made, not so much through lapse of memory as through an unaccountable addling of the brains. In short, I never yet encountered the mere mathematician who could be trusted out of equal roots, or one who did not clandestinely hold it as a point of his faith that x^2+px was absolutely and unconditionally equal to q. Say to one of these gentlemen, by way of experiment, if you please, that you believe occasions may occur where x^2+px is not altogether equal to q, and, having made him understand what you mean, get out of his reach as speedily as convenient, for, beyond doubt, he will endeavour to knock you down.

"I mean to say," continued Dupin, while I merely laughed at his last observations, "that if the Minister had been no more than a mathematician, the Prefect would have been under no necessity of giving me this check. I knew him, however, as both mathematician and poet, and my measures were adapted to his capacity with reference to the circumstances by which he was surrounded. I knew him as a courtier, too, and as a bold intriguant. Such a man, I considered, could not fail to be aware of the ordinary policial modes of action. He could not have failed to anticipate — and events have proved that he did not fail to anticipate — the waylayings to which he was subjected. He must have foreseen, I reflected, the secret investigations of his premises. His frequent absences from home at night, which were hailed by the Prefect as certain aids to his success, I regarded only as ruses to afford opportunity for thorough search to the police, and thus the sooner to impress them with the conviction, to which G—, in fact, did finally arrive, — the conviction that the letter was not upon the premises. I felt, also, that the whole train of thought, which I was at some pains in detailing to you just now, concerning the invariable principle of policial action in searches for articles concealed, — I felt that this whole train of thought would necessarily pass through the mind of the Minister. It would imperatively lead him to despise all the ordinary nooks of concealment. He could not, I reflected, be so weak as not to see that the most intricate and remote recess of his hotel would be as open as his commonest closets to the eyes, to the probes, to the gimlets, and to the microscopes of the Prefect. I saw, in fine, that he would be driven, as a matter of course, to simplicity, if not deliberately induced to it as a matter of choice. You will remember, perhaps, how desperately the Prefect laughed when I suggested, upon our first interview, that it was just possible this mystery troubled him so much on account of its being so very self-evident."

"Yes," said I, "I remember his merriment well. I really thought he would have fallen into convulsions."

"The material world," continued Dupin, "abounds with very strict analogies to the immaterial; and thus some colour of truth has been given to the rhetorical dogma that metaphor, or simile, may be made to strengthen an argument as well as to embellish a description. The principle of the *vis inertiæ*, for example, seems to be identical in physics and metaphysics. It is not more true in the former, that a large body is with more difficulty set in motion than a smaller one, and that its subsequent momentum is commensurate with this difficulty, than it is, in the latter, that intellects of the vaster capacity, while more forcible, more constant, and more eventful in their movements than those of inferior grade, are yet the less readily moved, and more embarrassed, and full of hesitation in the first few steps of their progress. Again: have you ever noticed which of the street signs, over the shop doors, are the most attractive of attention?"

"I have never given the matter a thought," I said.

"There is a game of puzzles," he resumed,

"which is played upon a map. One party playing requires another to find a given word, the name of town, river, state, or empire, — any word, in short, upon the motley and perplexed surface of the chart. A novice in the game generally seeks to embarrass his opponents by giving them the most minutely lettered names; but the adept selects such words as stretch, in large characters, from one end of the chart to the other. These, like the over-largely lettered signs and placards of the street, escape observation by dint of being excessively obvious; and here the physical oversight is precisely analogous with the moral inapprehension by which the intellect suffers to pass unnoticed those considerations which are too obtrusively and too palpably self-evident. But this is a point, it appears, somewhat above or beneath the understanding of the Prefect. He never once thought it probable, or possible, that the Minister had deposited the letter immediately beneath the nose of the whole world by way of best preventing any portion of that world from perceiving it.

"But the more I reflected upon the daring, dashing, and discriminating ingenuity of D—; upon the fact that the document must always have been at hand, if he intended to use it to good purpose; and upon the decisive evidence, obtained by the Prefect, that it was not hidden within the limits of that dignitary's ordinary search, the more satisfied I became that, to conceal this letter, the Minister had resorted to the comprehensive and sagacious expedient of not attempting to conceal it at all.

"Full of these ideas, I prepared myself with a pair of green spectacles, and called one fine morning, quite by accident, at the ministerial hotel. I found D— at home, yawning, lounging, and dawdling, as usual, and pretending to be in the last extremity of *ennui*. He is, perhaps, the most really energetic human being now alive; but that is only when nobody sees him.

"To be even with him, I complained of my weak eyes, and lamented the necessity of the spectacles under cover of which I cautiously and thoroughly surveyed the whole apartment, while seemingly intent only upon the conversation of my host.

"I paid especial attention to a large writing-table near which he sat, and upon which lay confusedly some miscellaneous letters and other papers, with one or two musical instruments and a few books. Here, however, after a long and very deliberate scrutiny, I saw nothing to excite particular suspicion.

"At length my eyes, in going the circuit of the room, fell upon a trumpery filigree card-rack of pasteboard, that hung dangling by a dirty blue ribbon from a little brass knob just beneath the middle of the mantelpiece. In this rack, which had three or four compartments, were five or six visiting-cards and a solitary letter. This last was much soiled and crumpled. It was torn nearly in two, across the middle, as if a design, in the first instance, to tear it entirely up as worthless, had been altered, or stayed, in the second. It had a large black seal, bearing the D— cipher very conspicuously, and was addressed, in a diminutive female hand, to D— " the Minister, himself. It was thrust carelessly, and even, as it seemed, contemptuously, into one of the uppermost divisions of the rack.

"No sooner had I glanced at this letter than I concluded it to be that of which I was in search. To be sure, it was, to all appearance, radically different from the one of which the Prefect had read us so minute a description. Here the seal was large and black, with the D— cipher, there it was small and red, with the ducal arms of the S— family. Here, the address, to the Minister, was diminutive and feminine; there the superscription, to a certain royal personage, was markedly bold and decided; the size alone formed a point of correspondence. But, then, the radicalness of these differences, which was excessive: the dirt; the soiled and torn condition of the paper, so inconsistent with the true methodical habits of D—, and so suggestive of a design to delude the beholder into an idea of the worthlessness of the document, — these things, together with the hyperobtrusive situation of this document, full in the view of every visitor, and thus exactly in accordance with the conclusions to which I had previously arrived; these things, I say, were strongly corroborative of suspicion, in one who came with the intention to suspect.

"I protracted my visit as long as possible, and, while I maintained a most animated discussion with the Minister upon a topic which I knew well had never failed to interest and excite him, I kept my attention really riveted upon the letter. In this examination, I committed to memory its external appearance and arrangement in the rack; and also fell, at length, upon a discovery which set at rest whatever trivial doubt I might have entertained. In scrutinizing the edges of the paper, I observed them to be more chafed than seemed necessary. They presented the broken appearance which is manifested when a stiff paper, having been once folded and pressed with a folder, is refolded in a reversed direction, in the same creases or edges which had formed the original fold. This discovery was sufficient. It was clear to me that the letter had been turned, as a glove, inside out, redirected and resealed. I bade the Minister good-morning, and took my departure at once, leaving a gold snuff-box upon the table.

"The next morning I called for the snuff-box, when we resumed, quite eagerly, the conversation of the preceding day. While thus engaged, however, a loud report, as if of a pistol, was heard immediately beneath the windows of the hotel, and was succeeded by a series of fearful screams, and the shoutings of a terrified mob. D— rushed to a casement, threw it open, and looked out. In the meantime I stepped to the card-rack, took the letter, put it in my pocket, and replaced it by a fac-simile (so far as regards externals) which I had carefully prepared at my lodgings, imitating the D— cipher very readily by means of a seal formed of bread.

"The disturbance in the street had been occasioned by the frantic behaviour of a man with a musket. He had fired it among a crowd of women and children. It proved, however, to have been without a ball, and the fellow was suffered to go his way as a lunatic or a drunkard. When he had gone, D— came from the window, whither I had followed him immediately upon securing the object in view. Soon afterward I bade him farewell. The pretended lunatic was a man in my own pay."

"But what purpose had you," I asked, "in replacing the letter by a fac-simile? Would it not have been better, at the first visit, to have seized it openly and departed?"

"D—," replied Dupin, "is a desperate man, and a man of nerve. His hotel, too, is not without attendants devoted to his interests. Had I made the wild attempt you suggest, I might never have left the ministerial presence alive. The good people of Paris might have heard of me no more. But I had an object apart from these considerations. You know my political prepossessions. In this matter, I act as a partisan of the lady concerned. For eighteen months the Minister has had her in his power. She has now him in hers, since, being unaware that the letter is not in his possession, he will proceed with his exactions as if it was. Thus will he inevitably commit himself, at once, to his political destruction. His downfall, too, will not be more precipitate than awkward. It is all very well to talk about the *facilis descensus Averni*; but in all kinds of climbing, as Catalani said of singing, it is far more easy to get up than to come down. In the present instance I have no sympathy, at least no pity, for him who descends. He is that *monstrum horrendum*, an unprincipled man of genius. I confess, however, that I should like very well to know the precise character of his thoughts, when, being defied by her whom the Prefect terms 'a certain personage,' he is reduced to opening the letter which I left for him in the card-rack."

"How? did you put anything particular in it?"

"Why, it did not seem altogether right to leave the interior blank; that would have been insulting. D—, at Vienna once, did me an evil turn, which I told him, quite good-humouredly, that I should remember. So, as I knew he would feel some curiosity in regard to the identity of the person who had outwitted him, I thought it a pity not to give him a clew. He is well acquainted with my MS., and I just copied into the middle of the blank sheet the words

"' — *Un dessein si funeste,*
S'il n'est digne d'Atrée, est digne de Thyeste.'

They are to be found in Crébillon's *Atrée*."

II. The Black Hand — Arthur B. Reeve

Kennedy and I had been dining rather late one evening at Luigi's, a little Italian restaurant on the lower West Side. We had known the place well in our student days, and had made a point of visiting it once a month since, in order to keep in practice in the fine art of gracefully handling long shreds of spaghetti. Therefore we did not think it strange when the proprietor himself stopped a moment at our table to greet us. Glancing furtively around at the other diners, mostly Italians, he suddenly leaned over and whispered to Kennedy:

"I have heard of your wonderful detective work, Professor. Could you give a little advice in the case of a friend of mine?"

"Surely, Luigi. What is the case?" asked Craig, leaning back in his chair.

Luigi glanced around again apprehensively and lowered his voice. "Not so loud, sir. When you pay your check, go out, walk around Washington Square, and come in at the private entrance. I'll be waiting in the hall. My friend is dining privately upstairs."

We lingered a while over our chianti, then quietly paid the check and departed.

True to his word, Luigi was waiting for us in the dark hall. With a motion that indicated silence, he led us up the stairs to the second floor, and quickly opened a door into what seemed to be a fair-sized private dining-room. A man was pacing the floor nervously. On a table was some food, untouched. As the door opened I thought he started as if in fear, and I am sure his dark face blanched, if only for an instant. Imagine our surprise at seeing Gennaro, the great tenor, with whom merely to have a speaking acquaintance was to argue oneself famous.

"Oh, it is you, Luigi," he exclaimed in perfect English, rich and mellow. "And who are these gentlemen?"

Luigi merely replied, "Friends," in English also, and then dropped off into a voluble, low-toned explanation in Italian.

I could see, as we waited, that the same idea had flashed over Kennedy's mind as over my own. It was now three or four days since the papers had reported the strange kidnapping of Gennaro's five-year-old daughter Adelina, his only child, and the sending of a demand for ten thousand dollars ransom, signed, as usual, with the mystic Black Hand — a name to conjure with in blackmail and extortion.

As Signor Gennaro advanced toward us, after his short talk with Luigi, almost before the introductions were over, Kennedy anticipated him by saying: "I understand, Signor, before you ask me. I have read all about it in the papers. You want someone to help you catch the criminals who are holding your little girl."

"No, no!" exclaimed Gennaro excitedly. "Not that. I want to get my daughter first. After that, catch them if you can — yes, I should like to have someone do it. But read this first and tell me what you think of it. How should I act to get my little Adelina back without harming a hair of her head?" The famous singer drew from a capacious pocket-book a dirty, crumpled letter, scrawled on cheap paper.

Kennedy translated it quickly. It read:

Honourable sir: Your daughter is in safe hands. But, by the saints, if you give this letter to the police as you did the other, not only she but your family also, someone near to you, will suffer. We will not fail as we did Wednesday. If you want your daughter back, go yourself, alone and without telling a soul, to Enrico Albano's Saturday night at the twelfth hour. You must provide yourself with $10,000 in bills hidden in Saturday's *Il Progresso Italiano*. In the back room you will see a man sitting alone at a table. He will have a red flower on his coat. You are to say, "A fine opera is 'I Pagliacci.'" If he answers, "Not without Gennaro," lay the newspaper down on the table. He will pick it up, leaving his own, the *Bolletino*. On the third page you will find written the place where your daughter has been left waiting for you. Go immediately and get her. But, by the God, if you have so much as the shadow of the police near Enrico's your daughter will be sent to you in a box that night. Do not fear to come. We pledge our word to deal fairly if you deal fairly. This is a last warning. Lest you shall forget we will show one other sign of our power tomorrow.

La Mano Nera.

The end of this letter was decorated with a skull and crossbones, a rough drawing of a dagger thrust through a bleeding heart, a coffin, and, under all, a huge black hand. There was no doubt about the type of letter. It was such as have of late years become increasingly common in all our large cities.

"You have not showed this to the police, I presume?" asked Kennedy.

"Naturally not."

"Are you going Saturday night?"

"I am afraid to go and afraid to stay away," was the reply, and the voice of the fifty-thousand-dollars-a-season tenor was as human as that of a five-dollar-a-week father, for at bottom all men, high or low, are one.

"'We will not fail as we did Wednesday,'" re-read Craig. "What does that mean?"

Gennaro fumbled in his pocketbook again, and at last drew forth a typewritten letter bearing the letterhead of the Leslie Laboratories, Incorporated.

"After I received the first threat," explained Gennaro, "my wife and I went from our apartments at the hotel to her father's, the banker Cesare, you know, who lives on Fifth Avenue. I gave the letter to the Italian Squad of the police. The next morning my father-in-law's butler noticed something peculiar about the milk. He barely touched some of it to his tongue, and he has been violently ill ever since. I at once sent the milk to the laboratory of my friend Doctor Leslie to have it analyzed. This letter shows what the household escaped."

"My dear Gennaro," read Kennedy. "The milk submitted to us for examination on the 10th inst. has been carefully analyzed, and I beg to hand you herewith the result:

"Specific gravity 1.036 at 15 degrees Cent.

Water	84.60	per	cent.
Casein	3.49	"	"
Albumin	.56	"	"
Globulin	1.32	"	"
Lactose	5.08	"	"
Ash	.72	"	"
Fat	3.42	"	"
Ricinus	1.19	"	"

"Ricinus is a new and little-known poison derived from the shell of the castor-oil bean. Professor Ehrlich states that one gram of the pure poison will kill 1,500,000 guinea pigs. Ricinus was lately isolated by Professor Robert, of Rostock, but is seldom found except in an impure state, though still very deadly. It surpasses strychnine, prussic acid, and other commonly known drugs. I congratulate you and yours on escaping and shall of course respect your wishes absolutely regarding keeping secret this attempt on your life. Believe me,

"Very sincerely yours,

"C. W. Leslie."

As Kennedy handed the letter back, he remarked significantly: "I can see very readily why you don't care to have the police figure in your case. It has got quite beyond ordinary police methods."

"And to-morrow, too, they are going to give another sign of their power," groaned Gennaro, sinking into the chair before his untasted food.

"You say you have left your hotel?" inquired Kennedy.

"Yes. My wife insisted that we would be more safely guarded at the residence of her father, the banker. But we are afraid even there since the poison attempt. So I have come here secretly to Luigi, my old friend Luigi, who is preparing food for us, and in a few minutes one of Cesare's automobiles will be here, and I will take the food up to her — sparing no expense or trouble. She is heartbroken. It will kill her, Professor Kennedy, if anything happens to our little Adelina.

"Ah, sir, I am not poor myself. A month's salary at the opera-house, that is what they ask of me. Gladly would I give it, ten thousand dollars — all, if they asked it, of my contract with Signor Cassinelli, the director. But the police — bah! — they are all for catching the villains. What good will it do me if they catch them and my little Adelina is returned to me dead? It is all very well for the Anglo-Saxon to talk of justice and the law, but I am — what you call it? — an emotional Latin. I want my little daughter — and at any cost. Catch the villains afterward — yes. I will pay double then to catch them so that they cannot blackmail me again. Only first I want my daughter back."

"And your father-in-law?"

"My father-in-law, he has been among you long enough to be one of you. He has fought them. He has put up a sign in his banking-house, 'No money paid on threats.' But I say it is foolish. I do not know

America as well as he, but I know this: the police never succeed — the ransom is paid without their knowledge, and they very often take the credit. I say, pay first, then I will swear a righteous vendetta — I will bring the dogs to justice with the money yet on them. Only show me how, show me how."

"First of all," replied Kennedy, "I want you to answer one question, truthfully, without reservation, as to a friend. I am your friend, believe me. Is there any person, a relative or acquaintance of yourself or your wife or your father-in-law, whom you even have reason to suspect of being capable of extorting money from you in this way? I needn't say that is the experience of the district attorney's office in the large majority of cases of this so-called Black Hand."

"No," replied the tenor without hesitation. "I know that, and I have thought about it. No, I can think of no one. I know you Americans often speak of the Black Hand as a myth coined originally by a newspaper writer. Perhaps it has no organization. But, Professor Kennedy, to me it is no myth. What if the real Black Hand is any gang of criminals who choose to use that convenient name to extort money? Is it the less real? My daughter is gone!"

"Exactly," agreed Kennedy. "It is not a theory that confronts you. It is a hard, cold fact. I understand that perfectly. What is the address of this Albano's?"

Luigi mentioned a number on Mulberry Street, and Kennedy made a note of it.

"It is a gambling saloon," explained Luigi. "Albano is a Neapolitan, a Camorrista, one of my countrymen of whom I am thoroughly ashamed, Professor Kennedy."

"Do you think this Albano had anything to do with the letter?"

Luigi shrugged his shoulders.

Just then a big limousine was heard outside. Luigi picked up a huge hamper that was placed in a corner of the room and, followed closely by Signor Gennaro, hurried down to it. As the tenor left us he grasped our hands in each of his.

"I have an idea in my mind," said Craig simply. "I will try to think it out in detail to-night. Where can I find you to-morrow?"

"Come to me at the opera-house in the afternoon, or if you want me sooner at Mr. Cesare's residence. Good night, and a thousand thanks to you, Professor Kennedy, and to you, also, Mr. Jameson. I trust you absolutely because Luigi trusts you."

We sat in the little dining-room until we heard the door of the limousine bang shut and the car shoot off with the rattle of the changing gears.

"One more question, Luigi," said Craig as the door opened again. "I have never been on that block in Mulberry Street where this Albano's is. Do you happen to know any of the shopkeepers on it or near it?"

"I have a cousin who has a drug store on the corner below Albano's, on the same side of the street."

"Good! Do you think he would let me use his store for a few minutes Saturday night — of course without any risk to himself?"

"I think I could arrange it."

"Very well. Then to-morrow, say at nine in the morning, I will stop here, and we will all go over to see him. Good night, Luigi, and many thanks for thinking of me in connection with this case. I've enjoyed Signor Gennaro's singing often enough at the opera to want to render him this service, and I'm only too glad to be able to be of service to all honest Italians; that is, if I succeed in carrying out a plan I have in mind."

A little before nine the following day Kennedy and I dropped into Luigi's again. Kennedy was carrying a suitcase which he had taken over from his laboratory to our rooms the night before. Luigi was waiting for us, and without losing a minute we sallied forth.

By means of the tortuous twists of streets in old Greenwich village we came out at last on Bleecker Street and began walking east amid the hurly-burly of races of lower New York. We had not quite reached Mulberry Street when our attention was attracted by a large crowd on one of the busy corners, held back by a cordon of police who were endeavouring to keep the people moving with that burly good nature which the six-foot Irish policeman displays toward the five-foot burden-bearers of southern and eastern Europe who throng New York.

Apparently, we saw, as we edged up into the front of the crowd, here was a building whose whole front had literally been torn off and wrecked. The thick plate-glass of the windows was smashed to a mass of greenish splinters on the sidewalk, while the windows of the upper floors and for several houses down the block in either street were likewise broken. Some thick iron bars which had formerly protected the windows were now bent and twisted. A huge hole yawned in the floor inside the doorway, and peering in we could see the desk and chairs a tangled mass of kindling.

"What's the matter?" I inquired of an officer near me, displaying my reporter's fire-line badge, more for its moral effect than in the hope of getting any real information in these days of enforced silence toward the press.

"Black Hand bomb," was the laconic reply.

"Whew!" I whistled. "Anyone hurt?"

"They don't usually kill anyone, do they?" asked the officer by way of reply to test my acquaintance with such things.

"No," I admitted. "They destroy more property than lives. But did they get anyone this time? This must have been a thoroughly overloaded bomb, I should judge by the looks of things."

"Came pretty close to it. The bank hadn't any more than opened when, bang! went this gas-pipe-and-dynamite thing. Crowd collected before the smoke had fairly cleared. Man who owns the bank was hurt, but not badly. Now come, beat it down to headquarters if you want to find out any more. You'll find it printed on the pink slips — the 'squeal book' — by this tune. 'Gainst the rules for me to talk," he added with a good-natured grin, then to the crowd: "Gwan, now. You're blockin' traffic. Keep movin'."

I turned to Craig and Luigi. Their eyes were riveted on the big gilt sign, half broken, and all askew overhead. It read:

CIRO DI CESARE & CO. BANKERS
NEW YORK, GENOA, NAPLES, ROME, PALERMO

"This is the reminder so that Gennaro and his father-in-law will not forget," I gasped.

"Yes," added Craig, pulling us away, "and Cesare himself is wounded, too. Perhaps that was for putting up the notice refusing to pay. Perhaps not. It's a queer case — they usually set the bombs off at night when no one is around. There must be more back of this than merely to scare Gennaro. It looks to me as if they were after Cesare, too, first by poison, then by dynamite."

We shouldered our way out through the crowd, and went on until we came to Mulberry Street, pulsing with life. Down we went past the little shops, dodging the children, and making way for women with huge bundles of sweat-shop clothing accurately balanced on their heads or hugged up under their capacious capes. Here was just one little colony of the hundreds of thousands of Italians — a population larger than the Italian population of Rome — of whose life the rest of New York knew and cared nothing.

At last we came to Albano's little wine-shop, a dark, evil, malodorous place on the street level of a five-story, alleged "new-law" tenement. Without hesitation Kennedy entered, and we followed, acting the part of a slumming party. There were a few customers at this early hour, men out of employment and an inoffensive-looking lot, though of course they eyed us sharply. Albano himself proved to be a greasy, low-browed fellow who had a sort of cunning look. I could well imagine such a fellow spreading terror in the hearts of simple folk by merely pressing both temples with his thumbs and drawing his long bony forefinger under his throat — the so-called Black Hand sign that has shut up many a witness in the middle of his testimony even in open court.

We pushed through to the low-ceilinged back room, which was empty, and sat down at a table. Over a bottle of Albano's famous California "red ink" we sat silently. Kennedy was making a mental note of the place. In the middle of the ceiling was a single gas-burner with a big reflector over it. In the back wall of the room was a horizontal oblong window, barred, and with a sash that opened like a transom. The tables were dirty and the chairs rickety. The walls were bare and unfinished, with beams innocent of decoration. Altogether it was as unprepossessing a place as I had ever seen.

Apparently satisfied with his scrutiny, Kennedy got up to go, complimenting the proprietor on his wine. I could see that Kennedy had made up his mind as to his course of action.

"How sordid crime really is," he remarked as we walked on down the street. "Look at that place of Albano's. I defy even the police news reporter on the *Star* to find any glamour in that."

Our next stop was at the corner at the little store kept by the cousin of Luigi, who conducted us back of the partition where prescriptions were compounded, and found us chairs.

A hurried explanation from Luigi brought a cloud to the open face of the druggist, as if he hesitated to lay himself and his little fortune open to the blackmailers. Kennedy saw it and interrupted.

"All that I wish to do," he said, "is to put in a little instrument here and use it to-night for a few minutes. Indeed, there will be no risk to you, Vincenzo. Secrecy is what I desire, and no one will ever know about it."

Vincenzo was at length convinced, and Craig opened his suit-case. There was little in it except several coils of insulated wire, some tools, a couple of packages wrapped up, and a couple of pairs of overalls. In a moment Kennedy had donned overalls and was smearing dirt and grease over his face and hands. Under his direction I did the same.

Taking the bag of tools, the wire, and one of the small packages, we went out on the street and then up through the dark and ill-ventilated hall of the tenement. Half-way up a woman stopped us suspiciously.

"Telephone company," said Craig curtly. "Here's permission from the owner of the house to string wires across the roof."

He pulled an old letter out of his pocket, but as it was too dark to read even if the woman had cared to do so, we went on up as he had expected, unmolested. At last we came to the roof, where there were some children at play a couple of houses down from us.

Kennedy began by dropping two strands of wire down to the ground in the back yard behind Vincenzo's shop. Then he proceeded to lay two wires along the edge of the roof.

We had worked only a little while when the children began to collect. However, Kennedy kept right on until we reached the tenement next to that in which Albano's shop was.

"Walter," he whispered, "just get the children away for a minute now."

"Look here, you kids," I yelled, "some of you will fall off if you get so close to the edge of the roof. Keep back."

It had no effect. Apparently they looked not a bit frightened at the dizzy mass of clothes-lines below us.

"Say, is there a candy store on this block?" I asked in desperation.

"Yes, sir," came the chorus.

"Who'll go down and get me a bottle of ginger ale?" I asked.

A chorus of voices and glittering eyes was the answer. They all would. I took a half-dollar from my pocket and gave it to the oldest.

"All right now, hustle along, and divide the change."

With the scamper of many feet they were gone, and we were alone. Kennedy had now reached Albano's, and as soon as the last head had disappeared below the scuttle of the roof he dropped two long strands down into the back yard, as he had done at Vincenzo's.

I started to go back, but he stopped me. "Oh, that will never do," he said. "The kids will see that the wires end here. I must carry them on several houses farther as a blind and trust to luck that they don't see the wires leading down below."

We were several houses down, still putting up wires when the crowd came shouting back, sticky with cheap trust-made candy and black with East

Side chocolate. We opened the ginger ale and forced ourselves to drink it so as to excite no suspicion, then a few minutes later descended the stairs of the tenement, coming out just above Albano's.

I was wondering how Kennedy was going to get into Albano's again without exciting suspicion. He solved it neatly.

"Now, Walter, do you think you could stand another dip into that red ink of Albano's?"

I said I might in the interests of science and justice — not otherwise.

"Well, your face is sufficiently dirty," he commented, "so that with the overalls you don't look very much as you did the first time you went in. I don't think they will recognize you. Do I look pretty good?"

"You look like a coal-heaver on the job," I said. "I can scarcely restrain my admiration."

"All right. Then take this little glass bottle. Go into the back room and order something cheap, in keeping with your looks. Then when you are all alone break the bottle. It is full of gas drippings. Your nose will dictate what to do next. Just tell the proprietor you saw the gas company's wagon on the next block and come up here and tell me."

I entered. There was a sinister-looking man, with a sort of unscrupulous intelligence, writing at a table. As he wrote and puffed at his cigar, I noticed a scar on his face, a deep furrow running from the lobe of his ear to his mouth. That, I knew, was a brand set upon him by the Camorra. I sat and smoked and sipped slowly for several minutes, cursing him inwardly more for his presence than for his evident look of the "*mala vita.*" At last he went out to ask the barkeeper for a stamp.

Quickly I tiptoed over to another corner of the room and ground the little bottle under my heel. Then I resumed my seat. The odor that pervaded the room was sickening.

The sinister-looking man with the scar came in again and sniffed. I sniffed. Then the proprietor came in and sniffed.

"Say," I said in the toughest voice I could assume, "you got a leak. Wait. I seen the gas company wagon on the next block when I came in. I'll get the man."

I dashed out and hurried up the street to the place where Kennedy was waiting impatiently. Rattling his tools, he followed me with apparent reluctance.

As he entered the wine-shop he snorted, after the manner of gasmen, "Where's de leak?"

"You find-a da leak," grunted Albano. "What-a you get-a you pay for? You want-a me do your work?"

"Well, half a dozen o' you wops get out o' here, that's all. D'youse all wanter be blown ter pieces wid dem pipes and cigarettes? Clear out," growled Kennedy.

They retreated precipitately, and Craig hastily opened his bag of tools.

"Quick, Walter, shut the door and hold it," exclaimed Craig, working rapidly. He unwrapped a little package and took out a round, flat disk-like thing of black vulcanized rubber. Jumping up on a table, he fixed it to the top of the reflector over the gas-jet.

"Can you see that from the floor, Walter?" he asked, under his breath.

"No," I replied, "not even when I know it is there."

Then he attached a couple of wires to it and led them across the ceiling toward the window, concealing them carefully by sticking them in the shadow of a beam. At the window he quickly attached the wires to the two that were dangling down from the roof and shoved them around out of sight.

"We'll have to trust that no one sees them," he said. "That's the best I can do at such short notice. I never saw a room so bare as this, anyway. There isn't another place I could put that thing without its being seen."

We gathered up the broken glass of the gas-drippings bottle, and I opened the door.

"It's all right now," said Craig, sauntering out before the bar. "Only de next time you has anyt'ing de matter call de company up. I ain't supposed to do dis wit'out orders, see?"

A moment later I followed, glad to get out of the oppressive atmosphere, and joined him in the back of Vincenzo's drug store, where he was again at work. As there was no back window there, it was quite a job to lead the wires around the outside from the back yard and in at a side window. It was at last done, however, without exciting suspicion, and Kennedy attached them to an oblong box of weathered oak and a pair of specially constructed dry batteries.

"Now," said Craig, as we washed off the stains of work and stowed the overalls back in the suitcase, "that is done to my satisfaction. I can tell Gennaro to go ahead safely now and meet the Black Handers."

From Vincenzo's we walked over toward Center Street, where Kennedy and I left Luigi to return to his restaurant, with instructions to be at Vincenzo's at half-past eleven that night.

We turned into the new police headquarters and went down the long corridor to the Italian Bureau. Kennedy sent in his card to Lieutenant Giuseppe in charge, and we were quickly admitted. The lieutenant was a short, full-faced fleshy Italian, with lightish hair and eyes that were apparently dull, until you suddenly discovered that that was merely a cover to their really restless way of taking in everything and fixing it on his mind, as if on a sensitive plate.

"I want to talk about the Gennaro case," began Craig. "I may add that I have been rather closely associated with Inspector O'Connor of the Central Office on a number of cases, so that I think we can trust each other. Would you mind telling me what you know about it if I promise you that I, too, have something to reveal?"

The lieutenant leaned back and watched Kennedy closely without seeming to do so. "When I was in Italy last year," he replied at length, "I did a good deal of work in tracing up some Camorra suspects. I had a tip about some of them to look up their records — I needn't say where it came from, but it was a good one. Much of the evidence against some of those fellows who are being tried at Viterbo was gathered by the Carabinieri as a result of hints that I was able to give them — clues that were furnished to me here in America from the source I speak of. I suppose there is really no need to conceal it, though. The original tip came from a certain banker here in New York."

"I can guess who it was," nodded Craig.

"Then, as you know, this banker is a fighter. He is the man who organized the White Hand — an organization which is trying to rid the Italian population of the Black Hand. His society had a lot of evidence regarding former members of both the Camorra in Naples and the Mafia in Sicily, as well as the Black Hand gangs in New York, Chicago, and other cities. Well, Cesare, as you know, is Gennaro's father-in-law.

"While I was in Naples looking up the record of a certain criminal I heard of a peculiar murder committed some years ago. There was an honest old music master who apparently lived the quietest and most harmless of lives. But it became known that he was supported by Cesare and had received handsome presents of money from him. The old man was, as you may have guessed, the first music teacher of Gennaro, the man who discovered him. One might have been at a loss to see how he could have an enemy, but there was one who coveted his small fortune. One day he was stabbed and robbed. His murderer ran out into the street, crying out that the poor man had been killed. Naturally a crowd rushed up in a moment, for it was in the middle of the day. Before the injured man could make it understood who had struck him the assassin was down the street and lost in the maze of old Naples where he well knew the houses of his friends who would hide him. The man who is known to have committed that crime — Francesco Paoli — escaped to New York. We are looking for him to-day. He is a clever man, far above the average — son of a doctor in a town a few miles from Naples, went to the university, was expelled for some mad prank — in short, he was the black sheep of the family. Of course over here he is too high-born to work with his hands on a railroad or in a trench, and not educated enough to work at anything else. So he has been preying on his more industrious countrymen — a typical case of a man living by his wits with no visible means of support.

"Now I don't mind telling you in strict confidence," continued the lieutenant, "that it's my theory that old Cesare had seen Paoli here, knew he was wanted for that murder of the old music master, and gave me the tip to look up his record. At any rate, Paoli disappeared right after I returned from Italy, and we haven't been able to locate him since. He must have found out in some way that the tip to look him up had been given by the White Hand. He had been a Camorrista, in Italy, and had many ways of getting information here in America."

He paused, and balanced a piece of cardboard in his hand.

"It is my theory of this case that if we could locate this Paoli we could solve the kidnapping of little Adelina Gennaro very quickly. That's his picture."

Kennedy and I bent over to look at it, and I started in surprise. It was my evil-looking friend with the scar on his cheek.

"Well," said Craig, quietly handing back the card, "whether or not he is the man, I know where we can catch the kidnappers to-night, Lieutenant."

It was Giuseppe's turn to show surprise now.

"With your assistance I'll get this man and the whole gang to-night," explained Craig, rapidly sketching over his plan and concealing just enough to make sure that no matter how anxious the lieutenant was to get the credit he could not spoil the affair by premature interference.

The final arrangement was that four of the best men of the squad were to hide in a vacant store across from Vincenzo's early in the evening, long before anyone was watching. The signal for them to appear was to be the extinguishing of the lights behind the coloured bottles in the druggist's window. A taxicab was to be kept waiting at headquarters at the same time with three other good men ready to start for a given address the moment the alarm was given over the telephone.

We found Gennaro awaiting us with the greatest anxiety at the opera house. The bomb at Cesare's had been the last straw. Gennaro had already drawn from his bank ten crisp one-thousand-dollar bills, and already he had a copy of *Il Progresso* in which he had hidden the money between the sheets.

"Mr. Kennedy," he said, "I am going to meet them to-night. They may kill me. See, I have provided myself with a pistol — I shall fight, too, if necessary for my little Adelina. But if it is only money they want, they shall have it."

"One thing I want to say," began Kennedy.

"No, no, no!" cried the tenor. "I will go — you shall not stop me."

"I don't wish to stop you," Craig reassured him.

"But one thing — do exactly as I tell you, and I swear not a hair of the child's head will be injured and we will get the blackmailers, too."

"How?" eagerly asked Gennaro. "What do you want me to do?"

"All I want you to do is to go to Albano's at the appointed time. Sit down in the back room. Get into conversation with them, and, above all, Signor, as soon as you get the copy of the *Bolletino* turn to the third page, pretend not to be able to read the address. Ask the man to read it. Then repeat it after him. Pretend to be overjoyed. Offer to set up wine for the whole crowd. Just a few minutes, that is all I ask, and I will guarantee that you will be the happiest man in New York to-morrow."

Gennaro's eyes filled with tears as he grasped Kennedy's hand. "That is better than having the whole police force back of me," he said. "I shall never forget, never forget."

As we went out Kennedy remarked: "You can't blame them for keeping their troubles to themselves. Here we send a police officer over to Italy to look up the records of some of the worst suspects. He loses his life. Another takes his place. Then after he gets back he is set to work on the mere clerical routine of translating them. One of his associates is reduced in rank. And so what does it all come to? Hundreds of records have become useless because the three years within which the criminals could be deported have elapsed with nothing done. Intelligent, isn't it? I believe it has been established that all but about fifty of seven hundred known Italian suspects are still at large, mostly in this city. And the rest of the Italian population is guarded from them by a squad of police in number scarcely one-thirtieth of the number of known criminals. No, it's our fault if the Black Hand thrives."

We had been standing on the corner of Broadway, waiting for a car.

"Now, Walter, don't forget. Meet me at the Bleecker Street station of the subway at eleven thirty. I'm off to the university. I have some very important experiments with phosphorescent salts that I want to finish to-day."

"What has that to do with the case?" I asked mystified.

"Nothing," replied Craig. "I didn't say it had. At eleven thirty, don't forget. By George, though, that Paoli must be a clever one — think of his knowing about ricinus. I only heard of it myself recently. Well, here's my car. Good-bye."

Craig swung aboard an Amsterdam Avenue car, leaving me to kill eight nervous hours of my weekly day of rest from the *Star*.

They passed at length, and at precisely the appointed time Kennedy and I met. With suppressed excitement, at least on my part, we walked over to Vincenzo's. At night this section of the city was indeed a black enigma. The lights in the shops where olive oil, fruit, and other things were sold, were winking out one by one; here and there strains of music floated out of wine-shops, and little groups lingered on corners conversing in animated sentences. We passed Albano's on the other side of the street, being careful not to look at it too closely, for several men were hanging idly about — pickets, apparently, with some secret code that would instantly have spread far and wide the news of any alarming action.

At the corner we crossed and looked in Vincenzo's window a moment, casting a furtive glance across the street at the dark empty store where the police must be hiding. Then we went in and casually sauntered back of the partition. Luigi was there already. There were several customers still in the store, however, and therefore we had to sit in silence while Vincenzo quickly finished a prescription and waited on the last one.

At last the doors were locked and the lights lowered, all except those in the windows which were to serve as signals.

"Ten minutes to twelve," said Kennedy, placing the oblong box on the table. "Gennaro will be going in soon. Let us try this machine now and see if it works. If the wires have been cut since we put them up this morning Gennaro will have to take his chances alone."

Kennedy reached over and with a light movement of his forefinger touched a switch.

Instantly a babel of voices filled the store, all talking at once, rapidly and loudly. Here and there we could distinguish a snatch of conversation, a word, a phrase, now and then even a whole sentence above the rest. There was the clink of glasses. I could hear the rattle of dice on a bare table, and an oath. A cork popped. Somebody scratched a match.

We sat bewildered, looking at Kennedy.

"Imagine that you are sitting at a table in Albano's back room," was all he said. "This is what you would be hearing. This is my 'electric ear' — in other words the dictagraph, used, I am told, by the Secret Service of the United States. Wait, in a moment you will hear Gennaro come in. Luigi and

Vincenzo, translate what you hear. My knowledge of Italian is pretty rusty."

"Can they hear us?" whispered Luigi in an awestruck whisper.

Craig laughed. "No, not yet. But I have only to touch this other switch, and I could produce an effect in that room that would rival the famous writing on Belshazzar's wall — only it would be a voice from the wall instead of writing."

"They seem to be waiting for someone," said Vincenzo. "I heard somebody say: 'He will be here in a few minutes. Now get out.'"

The babel of voices seemed to calm down as men withdrew from the room. Only one or two were left.

"One of them says the child is all right. She has been left in the back yard," translated Luigi.

"What yard? Did he say?" asked Kennedy.

"No, they just speak of it as the 'yard.'"

"Jameson, go outside in the store to the telephone booth and call up headquarters. Ask them if the automobile is ready, with the men in it."

I rang up, and after a moment the police central answered that everything was right.

"Then tell central to hold the line clear — we mustn't lose a moment. Jameson, you stay in the booth. Vincenzo, you pretend to be working around your window, but not in such a way as to attract attention, for they have men watching the street very carefully. What is it, Luigi?"

"Gennaro is coming. I just heard one of them

say, 'Here he comes.'"

Even from the booth I could hear the dictagraph repeating the conversation in the dingy little back room of Albano's, down the street.

"He's ordering a bottle of red wine," murmured Luigi, dancing up and down with excitement.

Vincenzo was so nervous that he knocked a bottle down in the window, and I believe that my heartbeats were almost audible over the telephone which I was holding, for the police operator called me down for asking so many times if all was ready.

"There it is — the signal," cried Craig. "'A fine opera is "I Pagliacci."' Now listen for the answer."

A moment elapsed, then, "Not without Gennaro," came a gruff voice in Italian from the dictagraph.

A silence ensued. It was tense.

"Wait, wait," said a voice which I recognized instantly as Gennaro's. "I cannot read this. What is this, 23½ Prince Street?"

"No, 33½. She has been left in the back yard."

"Jameson," called Craig, "tell them to drive straight to 33½, Prince Street. They will find the girl in the back yard — quick, before the Black-Handers have a chance to go back on their word."

I fairly shouted my orders to the police headquarters. "They're off," came back the answer, and I hung up the receiver.

"What was that?" Craig was asking of Luigi. "I didn't catch it. What did they say?"

"That other voice said to Gennaro, 'Sit down

52

while I count this.'"

"Sh! he's talking again."

"If it is a penny less than ten thousand or I find a mark on the bills I'll call to Enrico, and your daughter will be spirited away again," translated Luigi.

"Now, Gennaro is talking," said Craig. "Good — he is gaining time. He is a trump. I can distinguish that all right. He's asking the gruff-voiced fellow if he will have another bottle of wine. He says he will. Good. They must be at Prince Street now — we'll give them a few minutes more, not too much, for word will be back to Albano's like wildfire, and they will get Gennaro after all. Ah, they are drinking again. What was that, Luigi? The money is all right, he says? Now, Vincenzo, out with the lights!"

A door banged open across the street, and four huge dark figures darted out in the direction of Albano's.

With his finger Kennedy pulled down the other switch and shouted: "Gennaro, this is Kennedy! To the street! *Polizia! Polizia!*"

A scuffle and a cry of surprise followed. A second voice, apparently from the bar, shouted, "Out with the lights, out with the lights!"

Bang! went a pistol, and another.

The dictagraph, which had been all sound a moment before, was as mute as a cigar-box.

"What's the matter?" I asked Kennedy, as he rushed past me.

"They have shot out the lights. My receiving instrument is destroyed. Come on, Jameson; Vincenzo, stay back if you don't want to appear in this."

A short figure rushed by me, faster even than I could go. It was the faithful Luigi.

In front of Albano's an exciting fight was going on. Shots were being fired wildly in the darkness, and heads were popping out of tenement windows on all sides. As Kennedy and I flung ourselves into the crowd we caught a glimpse of Gennaro, with blood streaming from a cut on his shoulder, struggling with a policeman while Luigi vainly was trying to interpose himself between them. A man, held by another policeman, was urging the first officer on. "That's the man," he was crying. "That's the kidnapper. I caught him."

In a moment Kennedy was behind him. "Paoli, you lie. You are the kidnapper. Seize him — he has the money on him. That other is Gennaro himself."

The policeman released the tenor, and both of them seized Paoli. The others were beating at the door, which was being frantically barricaded inside.

Just then a taxicab came swinging up the street. Three men jumped out and added their strength to those who were battering down Albano's barricade.

Gennaro, with a cry, leaped into the taxicab. Over his shoulder I could see a tangled mass of dark brown curls, and a childish voice lisped: "Why didn't you come for me, papa? The bad man told me if I waited in the yard you would come for me. But if I cried he said he would shoot me. And I waited, and waited — "

"There, there, 'Lina, papa's going to take you straight home to mother."

A crash followed as the door yielded, and the famous Paoli gang was in the hands of the law.

III. The Bitter Bit — Wilkie Collins

Extracted from the Correspondence of the London Police.

FROM CHIEF INSPECTOR THEAKSTONE, OF THE DETECTIVE POLICE, TO SERGEANT BULMER, OF THE SAME FORCE.

London, 4th July, 18 —.

Sergeant Bulmer, — This is to inform you that you are wanted to assist in looking up a case of importance, which will require all the attention of an experienced member of the force. The matter of the robbery on which you are now engaged you will please to shift over to the young man who brings you this letter. You will tell him all the circumstances of the case, just as they stand; you will put him up to the progress you have made (if any) toward detecting the person or persons by whom the money has been stolen; and you will leave him to make the best he can of the matter now in your hands. He is to have the whole responsibility of the case, and the whole credit of his success if he brings it to a proper issue.

So much for the orders that I am desired to communicate to you.

A word in your ear, next, about this new man who is to take your place. His name is Matthew Sharpin, and he is to have the chance given him of dashing into our office at one jump — supposing he turns out strong enough to take it. You will naturally ask me how he comes by this privilege. I can only tell you that he has some uncommonly strong interest to back him in certain high quarters, which you and I had better not mention except under our breaths. He has been a lawyer's clerk, and he is wonderfully conceited in his opinion of himself, as well as mean and underhand to look at. According to his own account, he leaves his old trade and joins ours of his own free will and preference. You will no more believe that than I do. My notion is, that he has managed to ferret out some private information in connection with the affairs of one of his master's clients, which makes him rather an awkward customer to keep in the office for the future, and which, at the same time, gives him hold enough over his employer to make it dangerous to drive him into a corner by turning him away. I think the giving him this unheard-of chance among us is, in plain words, pretty much like giving him hush-money to keep him quiet. However that may be, Mr. Matthew Sharpin is to have the case now in your hands, and if he succeeds with it, he pokes his ugly nose into our office as sure as fate. I put you up to this, sergeant, so that you may not stand in your own light by giving the new man any cause to complain of you at headquarters, and remain yours,

Francis Theakstone.

FROM MR. MATTHEW SHARPIN TO CHIEF INSPECTOR THEAKSTONE.

London, 5th July, 18 —.

Dear Sir, — Having now been favoured with the necessary instructions from Sergeant Bulmer, I beg to remind you of certain directions which I have received relating to the report of my future proceedings which I am to prepare for examination at headquarters.

The object of my writing, and of your examining what I have written before you send it to the higher authorities, is, I am informed, to give me, as an untried hand, the benefit of your advice in case I want it (which I venture to think I shall not) at any stage of my proceedings. As the extraordinary circumstances of the case on which I am now engaged make it impossible for me to absent myself from the place where the robbery was committed until I have made some progress toward discovering the thief, I am necessarily precluded from consulting you personally. Hence the necessity of my writing down the various details, which might, perhaps, be better communicated by word of mouth. This, if I am not mistaken, is the position in which we are now placed. I state my own impressions on the subject in writing, in order that we may clearly understand each other at the outset; and have the honour to remain your obedient servant,

Matthew Sharpin.

FROM CHIEF INSPECTOR THEAKSTONE TO MR. MATTHEW SHARPIN.

London, 5th July, 18 —.

Sir, — You have begun by wasting time, ink, and paper. We both of us perfectly well knew the position we stood in toward each other when I sent you with my letter to Sergeant Bulmer. There was not the least need to repeat it in writing. Be so good as to employ your pen in future on the business actually in hand.

You have now three separate matters on which to write me. First, you have to draw up a statement of your instructions received from Sergeant Bulmer, in order to show us that nothing has escaped your memory, and that you are thoroughly acquainted with all the circumstances of the case which has been intrusted to you. Secondly, you are to inform me what it is you propose to do. Thirdly, you are to report every inch of your progress (if you make any) from day to day, and, if need be, from hour to hour as well. This is *your* duty. As to what *my* duty may be, when I want you to remind me of it, I will write and tell you so. In the mean time, I remain yours,

Francis Theakstone.

FROM MR. MATTHEW SHARPIN TO CHIEF INSPECTOR THEAKSTONE.

London, 6th July, 18 —.

Sir, — You are rather an elderly person, and, as such, naturally inclined to be a little jealous of men like me, who are in the prime of their lives and their faculties. Under these circumstances, it is my duty to be considerate toward you, and not to bear too hardly on your small failings. I decline, therefore, altogether to take offense at the tone of your letter; I give you the full benefit of the natural generosity of my nature; I sponge the very existence of your surly communication out of my memory — in short, Chief Inspector Theakstone, I forgive you, and proceed to business.

My first duty is to draw up a full statement of the instructions I have received from Sergeant Bulmer. Here they are at your service, according to my version of them.

At number Thirteen Rutherford Street, Soho, there is a stationer's shop. It is kept by one Mr. Yatman. He is a married man, but has no family. Besides Mr. and Mrs. Yatman, the other inmates in the house are a lodger, a young single man named Jay, who occupies the front room on the second floor — a shopman, who sleeps in one of the attics, and a servant-of-all-work, whose bed is in the back kitchen. Once a week a charwoman comes to help this servant. These are all the persons who, on ordinary occasions, have means of access to the interior of the house, placed, as a matter of course, at their disposal.

Mr. Yatman has been in business for many years, carrying on his affairs prosperously enough to realize a handsome independence for a person in his position. Unfortunately for himself, he endeavoured to increase the amount of his property by speculating.

He ventured boldly in his investments; luck went against him; and rather less than two years ago he found himself a poor man again. All that was saved out of the wreck of his property was the sum of two hundred pounds.

Although Mr. Yatman did his best to meet his altered circumstances, by giving up many of the luxuries and comforts to which he and his wife had been accustomed, he found it impossible to retrench so far as to allow of putting by any money from the income produced by his shop. The business has been declining of late years, the cheap advertising stationers having done it injury with the public. Consequently, up to the last week, the only surplus property possessed by Mr. Yatman consisted of the two hundred pounds which had been recovered from the wreck of his fortune. This sum was placed as a deposit in a joint-stock bank of the highest possible character.

Eight days ago Mr. Yatman and his lodger, Mr. Jay, held a conversation on the subject of the commercial difficulties which are hampering trade in all directions at the present time. Mr. Jay (who lives by supplying the newspapers with short paragraphs relating to accidents, offenses, and brief records of remarkable occurrences in general — who is, in short, what they call a penny-a-liner) told his landlord that he had been in the city that day and heard unfavourable rumours on the subject of the joint-stock banks. The rumours to which he alluded had already reached the ears of Mr. Yatman from other quarters, and the confirmation of them by his lodger had such an effect on his mind — predisposed as it was to alarm by the experience of his former losses — that he resolved to go at once to the bank and withdraw his deposit. It was then getting on toward the end of the afternoon, and he arrived just in time to receive his money before the bank closed.

He received the deposit in bank-notes of the following amounts: one fifty-pound note, three twenty-pound notes, six ten-pound notes, and six five-pound notes. His object in drawing the money in this form was to have it ready to lay out immediately in trifling loans, on good security, among the small tradespeople of his district, some of whom are sorely pressed for the very means of existence at the present time. Investments of this kind seemed to Mr. Yatman to be the most safe and the most profitable on which he could now venture.

He brought the money back in an envelope placed in his breast pocket, and asked his shopman, on getting home, to look for a small, flat, tin cash-box, which had not been used for years, and which, as Mr. Yatman remembered it, was exactly of the right size to hold the bank-notes. For some time the cash-box was searched for in vain. Mr. Yatman called to his wife to know if she had any idea where it was. The question was overheard by the servant-of-all-work, who was taking up the tea-tray at the time, and by Mr. Jay, who was coming downstairs on his way out to the theatre. Ultimately the cash-box was found by the shopman. Mr. Yatman placed the bank-notes in it, secured them by a padlock, and put the box in his coat pocket. It stuck out of the coat pocket a very little, but enough to be seen. Mr. Yatman remained at home, upstairs, all that evening. No visitors called. At eleven o'clock he went to bed, and put the cash-box under his pillow.

When he and his wife woke the next morning the box was gone. Payment of the notes was immediately stopped at the Bank of England, but no news of the money has been heard of since that time.

So far the circumstances of the case are perfectly clear. They point unmistakably to the conclusion that the robbery must have been committed by some person living in the house. Suspicion falls, therefore, upon the servant-of-all-work, upon the shopman, and upon Mr. Jay. The two first knew that the cash-box was being inquired for by their master, but did not know what it was he wanted to put into it. They would assume, of course, that it was money. They both had opportunities (the servant when she took away the tea, and the shopman when he came, after shutting up, to give the keys of the till to his master) of seeing the cash-box in Mr. Yatman's pocket, and of inferring naturally, from its position there, that he intended to take it into his bedroom with him at night.

Mr. Jay, on the other hand, had been told, during the afternoon's conversation on the subject of joint-stock banks, that his landlord had a deposit of two hundred pounds in one of them. He also knew that Mr. Yatman left him with the intention of drawing that money out; and he heard the inquiry for the cash-box afterward, when he was coming downstairs. He must, therefore, have inferred that the money was in the house, and that the cash-box was the receptacle intended to contain it. That he could have had any idea, however, of the place in which Mr. Yatman intended to keep it for the night is impossible, seeing that he went out before the box was found, and did not return till his landlord was in bed. Consequently, if he committed the robbery, he must have gone into the bedroom purely on speculation.

Speaking of the bedroom reminds me of the necessity of noticing the situation of it in the house, and the means that exist of gaining easy access to it at any hour of the night.

The room in question is the back room on the first floor. In consequence of Mrs. Yatman's constitutional nervousness on the subject of fire, which makes her apprehend being burned alive in her room, in case of accident, by the hampering of the lock if the key is turned in it, her husband has never been accustomed to lock the bedroom door. Both he and his wife are, by their own admission, heavy sleepers; consequently, the risk to be run by any evil-disposed persons wishing to plunder the bedroom was of the most trifling kind. They could enter the room by merely turning the handle of the door; and, if they moved with ordinary caution, there was no fear of their waking the sleepers inside. This fact is of importance. It strengthens our conviction that the money must have been taken by one of the inmates of the house, because it tends to show that the robbery, in this case, might have been committed by persons not possessed of the superior vigilance and running of the experienced thief.

Such are the circumstances, as they were related to Sergeant Bulmer when he was first called in to discover the guilty parties, and, if possible, to recover the lost bank-notes. The strictest inquiry which he could institute failed of producing the smallest fragment of evidence against any of the persons on whom suspicion naturally fell. Their language and behaviour on being informed of the robbery was perfectly consistent with the language and behaviour of innocent people. Sergeant Bulmer felt from the first that this was a case for private inquiry and secret observation. He began by recommending Mr. and Mrs. Yatman to affect a feeling of perfect confidence in the innocence of the persons living under their roof, and he then opened the campaign by employing himself in following the goings and comings, and in discovering the friends, the habits, and the secrets of the maid-of-all-work.

Three days and nights of exertion on his own part, and on that of others who were competent to assist his investigations, were enough to satisfy him that there was no sound cause for suspicion against the girl.

He next practised the same precaution in relation to the shopman. There was more difficulty and uncertainty in privately clearing up this person's character without his knowledge, but the obstacles were at last smoothed away with tolerable success; and, though there is not the same amount of certainty in this case which there was in the case of the girl, there is still fair reason for supposing that the shopman has had nothing to do with the robbery of the cash-box.

As a necessary consequence of these proceedings, the range of suspicion now becomes limited to the lodger, Mr. Jay.

When I presented your letter of introduction to Sergeant Bulmer, he had already made some inquiries on the subject of this young man. The result, so far, has not been at all favourable. Mr. Jay's habits are irregular; he frequents public houses, and seems to be familiarly acquainted with a great many dissolute characters; he is in debt to most of the tradespeople whom he employs; he has not paid his rent to Mr. Yatman for the last month; yesterday evening he came home excited by liquor, and last week he was seen talking to a prizefighter; in short, though Mr. Jay does call himself a journalist, in virtue of his penny-a-line contributions to the newspapers, he is a young man of low taste, vulgar manners, and bad habits. Nothing has yet been discovered in relation to him which redounds to his credit in the smallest degree.

I have now reported, down to the very last details, all the particulars communicated to me by Sergeant Bulmer. I believe you will not find an omission anywhere; and I think you will admit, though you are prejudiced against me, that a clearer statement of facts was never laid before you than the statement I have now made. My next duty is to tell you what I propose to do now that the case is confided to my hands.

In the first place, it is clearly my business to take up the case at the point where Sergeant Bulmer has left it. On his authority, I am justified in assuming that I have no need to trouble myself about the maid-of-all-work and the shopman. Their characters are now to be considered as cleared up. What remains to be privately investigated is the question of the guilt or innocence of Mr. Jay. Before we give up the notes for lost, we must make sure, if we can, that he knows nothing about them.

This is the plan that I have adopted, with the full approval of Mr. and Mrs. Yatman, for discovering whether Mr. Jay is or is not the person who has stolen the cash-box:

I propose to-day to present myself at the house in the character of a young man who is looking for lodgings. The back room on the second floor will be shown to me as the room to let, and I shall establish myself there to-night as a person from the country who has come to London to look for a situation in a respectable shop or office.

By this means I shall be living next to the room occupied by Mr. Jay. The partition between us is mere lath and plaster. I shall make a small hole in it, near the cornice, through which I can see what Mr. Jay does in his room, and hear every word that is said when any friend happens to call on him. Whenever he is at home, I shall be at my post of observation; whenever he goes out, I shall be after him. By employing these means of watching him, I believe I may look forward to the discovery of his secret — if he knows anything about the lost bank-notes — as to a dead certainty.

What you may think of my plan of observation I can not undertake to say. It appears to me to unite the invaluable merits of boldness and simplicity. Fortified by this conviction, I close the present communication with feelings of the most sanguine description in regard to the future, and remain your obedient servant,

> Matthew Sharpin.

FROM THE SAME TO THE SAME.

> 7th July.

Sir, — As you have not honoured me with any answer to my last communication, I assume that, in spite of your prejudices against me, it has produced the favourable impression on your mind which I ventured to anticipate. Gratified and encouraged beyond measure by the token of approval which your eloquent silence conveys to me, I proceed to report the progress that has been made in the course of the last twenty-four hours.

I am now comfortably established next door to Mr. Jay, and I am delighted to say that I have two holes in the partition instead of one. My natural sense of humour has led me into the pardonable extravagance of giving them both appropriate names. One I call my peep-hole, and the other my pipe-hole. The name of the first explains itself; the name of the second refers to a small tin pipe or tube inserted in the hole, and twisted so that the mouth of it comes close to my ear while I am standing at my post of observation. Thus, while I am looking at Mr. Jay through my peep-hole, I can hear every word that may be spoken in his room through my pipe-hole.

Perfect candour — a virtue which I have possessed from my childhood — compels me to acknowledge, before I go any farther, that the ingenious notion of adding a pipe-hole to my proposed peep-hole originated with Mrs. Yatman. This lady — a most intelligent and accomplished person, simple, and yet distinguished in her manners, has entered into all my little plans with an enthusiasm and intelligence which I can not too highly praise. Mr. Yatman is so cast down by his loss that he is quite incapable of affording me any assistance. Mrs. Yatman, who is evidently most tenderly attached to him, feels her husband's sad condition of mind even more acutely than she feels the loss of the money, and is mainly stimulated to exertion by her desire to assist in raising him from the miserable state of prostration into which he has now fallen.

"The money, Mr. Sharpin," she said to me yesterday evening, with tears in her eyes, "the money may be regained by rigid economy and strict attention to business. It is my husband's wretched state of mind that makes me so anxious for the discovery of the thief. I may be wrong, but I felt hopeful of success as soon as you entered the house; and I believe that, if the wretch who robbed us is to be found, you are the man to discover him." I accepted this gratifying compliment in the spirit in which it was offered, firmly believing that I shall be found, sooner or later, to have thoroughly deserved it.

Let me now return to business — that is to say, to my peep-hole and my pipe-hole.

I have enjoyed some hours of calm observation of Mr. Jay. Though rarely at home, as I understand from Mrs. Yatman, on ordinary occasions, he has been indoors the whole of this day. That is suspicious, to begin with. I have to report, further, that he rose at a late hour this morning (always a bad sign in a young man), and that he lost a great deal of time, after he was up, in yawning and complaining to himself of headache. Like other debauched characters, he ate little or nothing for breakfast. His next proceeding was to smoke a pipe — a dirty clay pipe, which a gentleman would have been ashamed to put between his lips. When he had done smoking he took out pen, ink, and paper, and sat down to write with a groan — whether of remorse for having taken the bank-notes, or of disgust at the task before him, I am unable to say. After writing a few lines (too far away from my peep-hole to give me a chance of reading over his shoulder), he leaned back in his chair, and amused himself by humming the tunes of popular songs. I recognized "My Mary Anne," "Bobbin' Around," and "Old Dog Tray," among other melodies. Whether these do or do not represent secret signals by which he communicates with his accomplices remains to be seen. After he had amused himself for some time by humming, he got up and began to walk about the room, occasionally stopping to add a sentence to the paper on his desk. Before long he went to a locked cupboard and opened it. I strained my eyes eagerly, in expectation of making a discovery. I saw him take something carefully out of the cupboard — he turned round — and it was only a pint bottle of brandy! Having drunk some of the liquor, this extremely indolent reprobate lay down on his bed again, and in five minutes was fast asleep.

After hearing him snoring for at least two hours, I was recalled to my peep-hole by a knock at his door. He jumped up and opened it with suspicious activity.

A very small boy, with a very dirty face, walked in, said, "Please, sir, they're waiting for you," sat down with his legs a long way from the ground, and instantly fell asleep! Mr. Jay swore an oath, tied a wet towel round his head, and, going back to his paper, began to cover it with, writing as fast as his fingers could move the pen. Occasionally getting up to dip the towel in water and tie it on again, he continued at this employment for nearly three hours; then folded up the leaves of writing, woke the boy, and gave them to him, with this remarkable expression: "Now, then, young sleepy-head, quick march! If you see the governor, tell him to have the money ready for me when I call for it." The boy grinned and disappeared. I was sorely tempted to follow "sleepy-head," but, on reflection, considered it safest still to keep my eye on the proceedings of Mr. Jay.

In half an hour's time he put on his hat and walked out. Of course, I put on my hat and walked out also. As I went downstairs I passed Mrs. Yatman going up. The lady has been kind enough to undertake, by previous arrangement between us, to search Mr. Jay's room while he is out of the way, and while I am necessarily engaged in the pleasing duty of following him wherever he goes. On the occasion to which I now refer, he walked straight to the nearest tavern, and ordered a couple of mutton-chops for his dinner. I placed myself in the next box to him, and ordered a couple of mutton-chops for my dinner. Before I had been in the room a minute, a young man of highly suspicious manners and appearance, sitting at a table opposite, took his glass of porter in his hand and joined Mr. Jay. I pretended to be reading the newspaper, and listened, as in duty bound, with all my might.

"Jack has been here inquiring after you," says the young man.

"Did he leave any message?" asks Mr. Jay.

"Yes," says the other. "He told me, if I met with

you, to say that he wished very particularly to see you to-night, and that he would give you a look in at Rutherford Street at seven o'clock."

"All right," says Mr. Jay. "I'll get back in time to see him."

Upon this, the suspicious-looking young man finished his porter, and saying that he was rather in a hurry, took leave of his friend (perhaps I should not be wrong if I said his accomplice?), and left the room.

At twenty-five minutes and a half past six — in these serious cases it is important to be particular about time — Mr. Jay finished his chops and paid his bill. At twenty-six minutes and three quarters I finished my chops and paid mine. In ten minutes more I was inside the house in Rutherford Street, and was received by Mrs. Yatman in the passage. That charming woman's face exhibited an expression of melancholy and disappointment which it quite grieved me to see.

"I am afraid, ma'am," says I, "that you have not hit on any little criminating discovery in the lodger's room?"

She shook her head and sighed. It was a soft, languid, fluttering sigh — and, upon my life, it quite upset me. For the moment I forgot business, and burned with envy of Mr. Yatman.

"Don't despair, ma'am," I said, with an insinuating mildness which seemed to touch her. "I have heard a mysterious conversation — I know of a guilty appointment — and I expect great things from my peep-hole and my pipe-hole to-night. Pray don't be alarmed, but I think we are on the brink of a discovery."

Here my enthusiastic devotion to business got the better part of my tender feelings. I looked — winked — nodded — left her.

When I got back to my observatory, I found Mr. Jay digesting his mutton-chops in an arm-chair, with his pipe in his mouth. On his table were two tumblers, a jug of water, and the pint bottle of brandy. It was then close upon seven o'clock. As the hour struck the person described as "Jack" walked in.

He looked agitated — I am happy to say he looked violently agitated. The cheerful glow of anticipated success diffused itself (to use a strong expression) all over me, from head to foot. With breathless interest I looked through my peep-hole, and saw the visitor — the "Jack" of this delightful case — sit down, facing me, at the opposite side of the table to Mr. Jay. Making allowance for the difference in expression which their countenances just now happened to exhibit, these two abandoned villains were so much alike in other respects as to lead at once to the conclusion that they were brothers. Jack was the cleaner man and the better dressed of the two. I admit that, at the outset. It is, perhaps, one of my failings to push justice and impartiality to their utmost limits. I am no Pharisee; and where Vice has its redeeming point, I say, let Vice have its due — yes, yes, by all manner of means, let Vice have its due.

"What's the matter now, Jack?" says Mr. Jay.

"Can't you see it in my face?" says Jack. "My dear fellow, delays are dangerous. Let us have done with suspense, and risk it, the day after to-morrow."

"So soon as that?" cries Mr. Jay, looking very

much astonished. "Well, I'm ready, if you are. But, I say, Jack, is somebody else ready too? Are you quite sure of that?"

He smiled as he spoke — a frightful smile — and laid a very strong emphasis on those two words, "Somebody else." There is evidently a third ruffian, a nameless desperado, concerned in the business.

"Meet us to-morrow," says Jack, "and judge for yourself. Be in the Regent's Park at eleven in the morning, and look out for us at the turning that leads to the Avenue Road."

"I'll be there," says Mr. Jay. "Have a drop of brandy and water? What are you getting up for? You're not going already?"

"Yes I am," says Jack. "The fact is, I'm so excited and agitated that I can't sit still anywhere for five minutes together. Ridiculous as it may appear to you, I'm in a perpetual state of nervous flutter. I can't, for the life of me, help fearing that we shall be found out. I fancy that every man who looks twice at me in the street is a spy — "

At these words I thought my legs would have given way under me. Nothing but strength of mind kept me at my peep-hole — nothing else, I give you my word of honour.

"Stuff and nonsense!" cries Mr. Jay, with all the effrontery of a veteran in crime. "We have kept the secret up to this time, and we will manage cleverly to the end. Have a drop of brandy and water, and you will feel as certain about it as I do."

Jack steadily refused the brandy and water, and steadily persisted in taking his leave.

"I must try if I can't walk it off," he said. "Remember to-morrow morning — eleven o'clock, Avenue Road, side of the Regent's Park."

With those words he went out. His hardened relative laughed desperately and resumed the dirty clay pipe.

I sat down on the side of my bed, actually quivering with excitement.

It is clear to me that no attempt has yet been made to change the stolen bank-notes, and I may add that Sergeant Bulmer was of that opinion also when he left the case in my hands. What is the natural conclusion to draw from the conversation which I have just set down? Evidently that the confederates meet to-morrow to take their respective shares in the stolen money, and to decide on the safest means of getting the notes changed the day after. Mr. Jay is, beyond a doubt, the leading criminal in this business, and he will probably run the chief risk — that of changing the fifty-pound note. I shall, therefore, still make it my business to follow him — attending at the Regent's Park to-morrow, and doing my best to hear what is said there. If another appointment is made for the day after, I shall, of course, go to it. In the meantime, I shall want the immediate assistance of two competent persons (supposing the rascals separate after their meeting) to follow the two minor criminals. It is only fair to add that, if the rogues all retire together, I shall probably keep my subordinates in reserve. Being naturally ambitious, I desire, if possible, to have the whole credit of discovering this robbery to myself.

8th July.

I have to acknowledge, with thanks, the speedy

arrival of my two subordinates — men of very average abilities, I am afraid; but, fortunately, I shall always be on the spot to direct them.

My first business this morning was necessarily to prevent possible mistakes by accounting to Mr. and Mrs. Yatman for the presence of two strangers on the scene. Mr. Yatman (between ourselves, a poor, feeble man) only shook his head and groaned. Mrs. Yatman (that superior woman) favoured me with a charming look of intelligence.

"Oh, Mr. Sharpin!" she said, "I am so sorry to see those two men! Your sending for their assistance looks as if you were beginning to be doubtful of success."

I privately winked at her (she is very good in allowing me to do so without taking offence), and told her, in my facetious way, that she laboured under a slight mistake.

"It is because I am sure of success, ma'am, that I send for them. I am determined to recover the money, not for my own sake only, but for Mr. Yatman's sake — and for yours."

I laid a considerable amount of stress on those last three words. She said, "Oh, Mr. Sharpin!" again, and blushed of a heavenly red, and looked down at her work. I could go to the world's end with that woman if Mr. Yatman would only die.

I sent off the two subordinates to wait until I wanted them at the Avenue Road gate of the Regent's Park. Half an hour afterward I was following the same direction myself at the heels of Mr. Jay.

The two confederates were punctual to the appointed time. I blush to record it, but it is nevertheless necessary to state that the third rogue — the nameless desperado of my report, or, if you prefer it, the mysterious "somebody else" of the conversation between the two brothers — is — a woman! and, what is worse, a young woman! and, what is more lamentable still, a nice-looking woman! I have long resisted a growing conviction that, wherever there is mischief in this world, an individual of the fair sex is inevitably certain to be mixed up in it. After the experience of this morning, I can struggle against that sad conclusion no longer. I give up the sex — excepting Mrs. Yatman, I give up the sex.

The man named "Jack" offered the woman his arm. Mr. Jay placed himself on the other side of her. The three then walked away slowly among the trees. I followed them at a respectful distance. My two subordinates, at a respectful distance also, followed me.

It was, I deeply regret to say, impossible to get near enough to them to overhear their conversation without running too great a risk of being discovered. I could only infer from their gestures and actions that they were all three talking with extraordinary earnestness on some subject which deeply interested them. After having been engaged in this way a full quarter of an hour, they suddenly turned round to retrace their steps. My presence of mind did not forsake me in this emergency. I signed to the two subordinates to walk on carelessly and pass them, while I myself slipped dexterously behind a tree. As they came by me, I heard "Jack" address these words to Mr. Jay:

"Let us say half past ten to-morrow morning. And mind you come in a cab. We had better not risk taking one in this neighbourhood."

Mr. Jay made some brief reply which I could not overhear. They walked back to the place at which they had met, shaking hands there with an audacious cordiality which it quite sickened me to see. They then separated. I followed Mr. Jay. My subordinates paid the same delicate attention to the other two.

Instead of taking me back to Rutherford Street, Mr. Jay led me to the Strand. He stopped at a dingy, disreputable-looking house, which, according to the inscription over the door, was a newspaper office, but which, in my judgment, had all the external appearance of a place devoted to the reception of stolen goods.

After remaining inside for a few minutes, he came out whistling, with his finger and thumb in his waistcoat pocket. Some men would now have arrested him on the spot. I remembered the necessity of catching the two confederates, and the importance of not interfering with the appointment that had been made for the next morning. Such coolness as this, under trying circumstances, is rarely to be found, I should imagine, in a young beginner, whose reputation as a detective policeman is still to make.

From the house of suspicious appearance Mr. Jay betook himself to a cigar-divan, and read the magazines over a cheroot. From the divan he strolled to the tavern and had his chops. I strolled to the tavern and had my chops. When he had done he went back to his lodging. When I had done I went back to mine. He was overcome with drowsiness early in the evening, and went to bed. As soon as I heard him snoring, I was overcome with drowsiness and went to bed also.

Early in the morning my two subordinates came to make their report.

They had seen the man named "Jack" leave the woman at the gate of an apparently respectable villa residence not far from the Regent's Park. Left to himself, he took a turning to the right, which led to a sort of suburban street, principally inhabited by shopkeepers. He stopped at the private door of one of the houses, and let himself in with his own key — looking about him as he opened the door, and staring suspiciously at my men as they lounged along on the opposite side of the way. These were all the particulars which the subordinates had to communicate. I kept them in my room to attend on me, if needful, and mounted to my peep-hole to have a look at Mr. Jay.

He was occupied in dressing himself, and was taking extraordinary pains to destroy all traces of the natural slovenliness of his appearance. This was precisely what I expected. A vagabond like Mr. Jay knows the importance of giving himself a respectable look when he is going to run the risk of changing a stolen bank-note. At five minutes past ten o'clock he had given the last brush to his shabby hat and the last scouring with bread-crumb to his dirty gloves. At ten minutes past ten he was in the street, on his way to the nearest cab-stand, and I and my subordinates were close on his heels.

He took a cab, and we took a cab. I had not overheard them appoint a place of meeting when following them in the Park on the previous day, but I soon found that we were proceeding in the old direction of the Avenue Road gate. The cab in which Mr. Jay was riding turned into the Park slowly. We stopped outside, to avoid exciting suspicion. I got out to follow the cab on foot. Just as I did so, I saw it stop, and detected the two confederates approaching it from among the trees. They got in, and the cab was turned about directly. I ran back to my own cab, and told the driver to let them pass him, and then to follow as before.

The man obeyed my directions, but so clumsily as to excite their suspicions. We had been driving after them about three minutes (returning along the road by which we had advanced) when I looked out of the window to see how far they might be ahead of us. As I did this, I saw two hats popped out of the windows of their cab, and two faces looking back at me. I sank into my place in a cold sweat; the expression is coarse, but no other form of words can describe my condition at that trying moment.

"We are found out!" I said, faintly, to my two subordinates. They stared at me in astonishment. My feelings changed instantly from the depth of despair to the height of indignation.

"It is the cabman's fault. Get out, one of you," I said, with dignity — "get out, and punch his head."

Instead of following my directions (I should wish this act of disobedience to be reported at headquarters) they both looked out of the window. Before I could express my just indignation, they both grinned, and said to me, "Please to look out, sir!"

I did look out. Their cab had stopped.

Where?

At a church door!

What effect this discovery might have had upon the ordinary run of men I don't know. Being of a strong religious turn myself, it filled me with horror. I have often read of the unprincipled cunning of criminal persons, but I never before heard of three thieves attempting to double on their pursuers by entering a church! The sacrilegious audacity of that proceeding is, I should think, unparalleled in the annals of crime.

I checked my grinning subordinates by a frown. It was easy to see what was passing in their superficial minds. If I had not been able to look below the surface, I might, on observing two nicely-dressed men and one nicely-dressed woman enter a church before eleven in the morning on a week day, have come to the same hasty conclusion at which my inferiors had evidently arrived. As it was, appearances had no power to impose on *me*. I got out, and, followed by one of my men, entered the church. The other man I sent round to watch the vestry door. You may catch a weasel asleep, but not your humble servant, Matthew Sharpin!

We stole up the gallery stairs, diverged to the organ-loft, and peered through the curtains in front. There they were, all three, sitting in a pew below — yes, incredible as it may appear, sitting in a pew below!

Before I could determine what to do, a clergyman made his appearance in full canonicals from the vestry door, followed by a clerk. My brain whirled and my eyesight grew dim. Dark remembrances of robberies committed in vestries floated through my mind. I trembled for the excellent man in full canonicals — I even trembled for the clerk.

The clergyman placed himself inside the altar rails. The three desperadoes approached him. He opened his book, and began to read. What? you will ask.

I answer, without the slightest hesitation, the first lines of the Marriage Service.

My subordinate had the audacity to look at me, and then to stuff his pocket-handkerchief into his mouth. I scorned to pay any attention to him. After I had discovered that the man "Jack" was the bridegroom, and that the man Jay acted the part of father, and gave away the bride, I left the church, followed by my men, and joined the other subordinate outside the vestry door. Some people in my position would now have felt rather crestfallen, and would have begun to think that they had made a very foolish mistake. Not the faintest misgiving of any kind troubled me. I did not feel in the slightest degree depreciated in my own estimation. And even now, after a lapse of three hours, my mind remains, I am happy to say, in the same calm and hopeful condition.

As soon as I and my subordinates were assembled together outside the church, I intimated my intention of still following the other cab in spite of what had occurred. My reason for deciding on this course will appear presently. The two subordinates appeared to be astonished at my resolution. One of them had the impertinence to say to me,

"If you please, sir, who is it that we are after? A man who has stolen money, or a man who has stolen a wife?"

The other low person encouraged him by laughing. Both have deserved an official reprimand, and both, I sincerely trust, will be sure to get it.

When the marriage ceremony was over, the three got into their cab, and once more our vehicle (neatly hidden round the corner of the church)

started to follow theirs.

We traced them to the terminus of the South-western Railway. The newly-married couple took tickets for Richmond, paying their fare with a half sovereign, and so depriving me of the pleasure of arresting them, which I should certainly have done if they had offered a banknote. They parted from Mr. Jay, saying, "Remember the address — 14 Babylon Terrace. You dine with us to-morrow week." Mr. Jay accepted the invitation, and added, jocosely, that he was going home at once to get off his clean clothes, and to be comfortable and dirty again for the rest of the day. I have to report that I saw him home safely, and that he is comfortable and dirty again (to use his own disgraceful language) at the present moment.

Here the affair rests, having by this time reached what I may call its first stage.

I know very well what persons of hasty judgment will be inclined to say of my proceedings thus far. They will assert that I have been deceiving myself all through in the most absurd way; they will declare that the suspicious conversations which I have reported referred solely to the difficulties and dangers of successfully carrying out a runaway match; and they will appeal to the scene in the church as offering undeniable proof of the correctness of their assertions. So let it be. I dispute nothing up to this point. But I ask a question, out of the depths of my own sagacity as a man of the world, which the bitterest of my enemies will not, I think, find it particularly easy to answer.

Granted the fact of the marriage, what proof does it afford me of the innocence of the three persons concerned in that clandestine transaction? It gives me none. On the contrary, it strengthens my suspicions against Mr. Jay and his confederates, because it suggests a distinct motive for their stealing the money. A gentleman who is going to spend his honeymoon at Richmond wants money; and a gentleman who is in debt to all his tradespeople wants money. Is this an unjustifiable imputation of bad motives? In the name of outraged Morality, I deny it. These men have combined together, and have stolen a woman. Why should they not combine together and steal a cash-box? I take my stand on the logic of rigid Virtue, and I defy all the sophistry of Vice to move me an inch out of my position.

Speaking of virtue, I may add that I have put this view of the case to Mr. and Mrs. Yatman. That accomplished and charming woman found it difficult at first to follow the close chain of my reasoning. I am free to confess that she shook her head, and shed tears, and joined her husband in premature lamentation over the loss of the two hundred pounds. But a little careful explanation on my part, and a little attentive listening on hers, ultimately changed her opinion. She now agrees with me that there is nothing in this unexpected circumstance of the clandestine marriage which absolutely tends to divert suspicion from Mr. Jay, or Mr. "Jack," or the runaway lady. "Audacious hussy" was the term my fair friend used in speaking of her; but let that pass. It is more to the purpose to record that Mrs. Yatman has not lost confidence in me, and that Mr. Yatman promises to follow her example, and do his best to look hopefully for future results.

I have now, in the new turn that circumstances have taken, to await advice from your office. I pause for fresh orders with all the composure of a man who has got two strings to his bow. When I traced the three confederates from the church door to the railway terminus, I had two motives for doing so. First, I followed them as a matter of official business, believing them still to have been guilty of the robbery. Secondly, I followed them as a matter of private speculation, with a view of discovering the place of refuge to which the runaway couple intended to retreat, and of making my information a marketable commodity to offer to the young lady's family and friends. Thus, whatever happens, I may congratulate myself beforehand on not having wasted my time. If the office approves of my conduct, I have my plan ready for further proceedings. If the office blames me, I shall take myself off, with my marketable information, to the genteel villa residence in the neighbourhood of the Regent's Park. Any way, the affair puts money into my pocket, and does credit to my penetration as an uncommonly sharp man.

I have only one word more to add, and it is this: If any individual ventures to assert that Mr. Jay and his confederates are innocent of all share in the stealing of the cash-box, I, in return, defy that individual — though he may even be the Chief Inspector Theakstone himself — to tell me who has committed the robbery at Rutherford Street, Soho.

Strong in that conviction, I have the honour to be your very obedient servant,

Matthew Sharpin.

FROM CHIEF INSPECTOR THEAKSTONE TO SERGEANT BULMER.

Birmingham, July 9th.

Sergeant Bulmer, — That empty-headed puppy, Mr. Matthew Sharpin, has made a mess of the case at Rutherford Street, exactly as I expected he would. Business keeps me in this town, so I write to you to set the matter straight. I inclose with this the pages of feeble scribble-scrabble which the creature Sharpin calls a report. Look them over; and when you have made your way through all the gabble, I think you will agree with me that the conceited booby has looked for the thief in every direction but the right one. You can lay your hand on the guilty person in five minutes, now. Settle the case at once; forward your report to me at this place, and tell Mr. Sharpin that he is suspended till further notice.

Yours,

Francis Theakstone.

FROM SERGEANT BULMER TO CHIEF INSPECTOR THEAKSTONE.

London, July 10th.

Inspector Theakstone, — Your letter and inclosure came safe to hand. Wise men, they say, may always learn something even from a fool. By the time I had got through Sharpin's maundering report of his own folly, I saw my way clear enough to the end of the Rutherford Street case, just as you thought I should. In half an hour's time I was at the house. The first person I saw there was Mr. Sharpin himself.

"Have you come to help me?" says he.

"Not exactly," says I. "I've come to tell you that you are suspended till further notice."

"Very good," says he, not taken down by so much as a single peg in his own estimation. "I thought you would be jealous of me. It's very natural; and I don't blame you. Walk in, pray, and make yourself at home. I'm off to do a little detective business on my own account, in the neighbourhood of the Regent's Park. Ta-ta, sergeant, ta-ta!"

With those words he took himself out of the way, which was exactly what I wanted him to do.

As soon as the maid-servant had shut the door, I told her to inform her master that I wanted to say a word to him in private. She showed me into the parlour behind the shop, and there was Mr. Yatman all alone, reading the newspaper.

"About this matter of the robbery, sir," says I.

He cut me short, peevishly enough, being naturally a poor, weak, womanish sort of man. "Yes, yes, I know," says he. "You have come to tell me that your wonderfully clever man, who has bored holes in my second-floor partition, has made a mistake, and is off the scent of the scoundrel who has stolen my money."

"Yes, sir," says I. "That *is* one of the things I came to tell you. But I have got something else to say besides that."

"Can you tell me who the thief is?" says he more pettish than ever.

"Yes, sir," says I, "I think I can."

He put down the newspaper, and began to look rather anxious and frightened.

"Not my shopman?" says he. "I hope, for the man's own sake, it's not my shopman."

"Guess again, sir," says I.

"That idle slut, the maid?" says he.

"She is idle, sir," says I, "and she is also a slut; my first inquiries about her proved as much as that. But she's not the thief."

"Then, in the name of heaven, who is?" says he.

"Will you please to prepare yourself for a very disagreeable surprise, sir?" says I. "And, in case you lose your temper, will you excuse remarking that I am the stronger man of the two, and that, if you allow yourself to lay hands on me, I may unintentionally hurt you, in pure self-defence."

He turned as pale as ashes, and pushed his chair two or three feet away from me.

"You have asked me to tell you, sir, who has taken your money," I went on. "If you insist on my giving you an answer — "

"I do insist," he said, faintly. "Who has taken it?"

"Your wife has taken it," I said, very quietly, and very positively at the same time.

He jumped out of the chair as if I had put a knife into him, and struck his fist on the table so heavily that the wood cracked again.

"Steady, sir," says I. "Flying into a passion won't help you to the truth."

"It's a lie!" says he, with another smack of his fist on the table — "a base, vile, infamous lie! How dare you — "

He stopped, and fell back into the chair again, looked about him in a bewildered way, and ended by bursting out crying.

"When your better sense comes back to you, sir," says I, "I am sure you will be gentleman enough to make an apology for the language you have just used. In the mean time, please to listen, if you can, to a word of explanation. Mr. Sharpin has sent in a report to our inspector of the most irregular and ridiculous kind, setting down not only all his own foolish doings and sayings, but the doings and sayings of Mrs. Yatman as well. In most cases, such a document would have been fit only for the wastepaper basket; but in this particular case it so happens that Mr. Sharpin's budget of nonsense leads to a certain conclusion, which the simpleton of a writer has been quite innocent of suspecting from the beginning to the end. Of that conclusion I am so sure that I will forfeit my place if it does not turn out that Mrs. Yatman has been practising upon the folly and conceit of this young man, and that she has tried to shield herself from discovery by purposely encouraging him to suspect the wrong persons. I tell you that confidently; and I will even go farther. I will undertake to give a decided opinion as to why Mrs. Yatman took the money, and what she has done with it, or with a part of it. Nobody can look at that lady, sir, without being struck by the great taste and beauty of her dress — "

As I said those last words, the poor man seemed to find his powers of speech again. He cut me short directly as haughtily as if he had been a duke instead of a stationer.

"Try some other means of justifying your vile calumny against my wife," says he. "Her milliner's bill for the past year is on my file of receipted accounts at this moment."

"Excuse me, sir," says I, "but that proves nothing. Milliners, I must tell you, have a certain rascally custom which comes within the daily experience of our office. A married lady who wished it can keep two accounts at her dressmaker's: one is the account which her husband sees and pays; the other is the private account, which contains all the extravagant items, and which the wife pays secretly, by installments, whenever she can. According to our usual experience, these installments are mostly squeezed out of the housekeeping money. In your case, I suspect, no installments have been paid; proceedings have been threatened; Mrs. Yatman, knowing your altered circumstances, has felt herself driven into a corner, and she has paid her private account out of your cash-box."

"I won't believe it," says he. "Every word you speak is an abominable insult to me and to my wife."

"Are you man enough, sir," says I, taking him up short, in order to save time and words, "to get that receipted bill you spoke of just now off the file, and come with me at once to the milliner's shop where Mrs. Yatman deals?"

He turned red in the face at that, got the bill directly, and put on his hat. I took out of my pocket-book the list containing the numbers of the lost notes, and we left the house together immediately.

Arrived at the milliner's (one of the expensive

West-end houses, as I expected), I asked for a private interview, on important business, with the mistress of the concern. It was not the first time that she and I had met over the same delicate investigation. The moment she set eyes on me she sent for her husband. I mentioned who Mr. Yatman was, and what we wanted.

"This is strictly private?" inquires the husband. I nodded my head.

"And confidential?" says the wife. I nodded again.

"Do you see any objection, dear, to obliging the sergeant with a sight of the books?" says her husband.

"None in the world, love, if you approve of it," says the wife.

All this while poor Mr. Yatman sat looking the picture of astonishment and distress, quite out of place at our polite conference. The books were brought, and one minute's look at the pages in which Mrs. Yatman's name figured was enough, and more than enough, to prove the truth of every word that I had spoken.

There, in one book, was the husband's account which Mr. Yatman had settled; and there, in the other, was the private account, crossed off also, the date of settlement being the very day after the loss of the cash-box. This said private account amounted to the sum of a hundred and seventy-five pounds, odd shillings, and it extended over a period of three years. Not a single installment had been paid on it. Under the last line was an entry to this effect: "Written to for the third time, June 23d." I pointed to it, and asked the milliner if that meant "last June." Yes, it did mean last June; and she now deeply regretted to say that it had been accompanied by a threat of legal proceedings.

"I thought you gave good customers more than three years' credit?" says I.

The milliner looks at Mr. Yatman, and whispers to me, "Not when a lady's husband gets into difficulties."

She pointed to the account as she spoke. The entries after the time when Mr. Yatman's circumstances became involved were just as extravagant for a person in his wife's situation, as the entries for the year before that period. If the lady had economized in other things, she had certainly not economized in the matter of dress.

There was nothing left now but to examine the cash-book, for form's sake. The money had been paid in notes, the amounts and numbers of which exactly tallied with the figures set down in my list.

After that, I thought it best to get Mr. Yatman out of the house immediately. He was in such a pitiable condition that I called a cab and accompanied him home in it. At first he cried and raved like a child; but I soon quieted him; and I must add, to his credit, that he made me a most handsome apology for his language as the cab drew up at his house door. In return, I tried to give him some advice about how to set matters right for the future with his wife. He paid very little attention to me, and went up stairs muttering to himself about a separation. Whether Mrs. Yatman will come cleverly out of the scrape or not seems doubtful. I should say myself that she would go into screeching hysterics, and so frighten the poor man into forgiving her. But this is no business of ours. So far as we are concerned, the case is now at an end, and the present report may come to a conclusion along with it.

I remain, accordingly, yours to command,

Thomas Bulmer.

P.S. — I have to add that, on leaving Rutherford Street, I met Mr. Matthew Sharpin coming to pack up his things.

"Only think!" says he, rubbing his hands in great spirits, "I've been to the genteel villa residence, and the moment I mentioned my business they kicked me out directly. There were two witnesses of the assault, and it's worth a hundred pounds to me if it's worth a farthing."

"I wish you joy of your luck," says I.

"Thank you," says he. "When may I pay you the same compliment on finding the thief?"

"Whenever you like," says I, "for the thief is found."

"Just what I expected," says he. "I've done all the work, and now you cut in and claim all the credit — Mr. Jay, of course."

"No," says I.

"Who is it then?" says he.

"Ask Mrs. Yatman," says I. "She's waiting to tell you."

"All right! I'd much rather hear it from that charming woman than from you," says he, and goes into the house in a mighty hurry.

What do you think of that, Inspector Theakstone? Would you like to stand in Mr. Sharpin's shoes? I shouldn't, I can promise you.

FROM CHIEF INSPECTOR THEAKSTONE TO MR. MATTHEW SHARPIN.

July 12th.

Sir, — Sergeant Bulmer has already told you to consider yourself suspended until further notice. I have now authority to add that your services as a member of the Detective Police are positively declined. You will please to take this letter as notifying officially your dismissal from the force.

I may inform you, privately, that your rejection is not intended to cast any reflections on your character. It merely implies that you are not quite sharp enough for our purposes. If we *are* to have a new recruit among us, we should infinitely prefer Mrs. Yatman.

Your obedient servant,

Francis Theakstone.

NOTE ON THE PRECEDING CORRESPONDENCE, ADDED BY MR. THEAKSTONE.

The inspector is not in a position to append any explanation of importance to the last of the letters. It has been discovered that Mr. Matthew Sharpin left the house in Rutherford Street five minutes after his interview outside of it with Sergeant Bulmer, his manner expressing the liveliest emotions of terror and astonishment, and his left cheek displaying a bright patch of red, which looked as if it might have been the result of what is popularly termed a smart box on the ear. He was also heard by the shopman at Rutherford Street to use a very shocking expression in reference to Mrs. Yatman, and was seen to clench his fist vindictively as he ran round the corner of the street. Nothing more has been heard of him; and it is conjectured that he has left London with the intention of offering his valuable services to the provincial police.

On the interesting domestic subject of Mr. and Mrs. Yatman still less is known. It has, however, been positively ascertained that the medical attendant of the family was sent for in a great hurry on the day when Mr. Yatman returned from the milliner's shop. The neighbouring chemist received, soon afterward, a prescription of a soothing nature to make up for Mrs. Yatman. The day after, Mr. Yatman purchased some smelling-salts at the shop, and afterward appeared at the circulating library to ask for a novel descriptive of high life that would amuse an invalid lady. It has been inferred from these circumstances that he has not thought it desirable to carry out his threat of separating from his wife, at least in the present (presumed) condition of that lady's sensitive nervous system.

IV. Missing: Page Thirteen — Anna Katherine Green

I

"One more! just one more well-paying affair, and I promise to stop; really and truly to stop."

"But, Puss, why one more? You have earned the amount you set for yourself, — or very nearly, — and though my help is not great, in three months I can add enough — "

"No, you cannot, Arthur. You are doing well; I appreciate it; in fact, I am just delighted to have you work for me in the way you do, but you cannot, in your position, make enough in three months, or in six, to meet the situation as I see it. Enough does not satisfy me. The measure must be full, heaped up, and running over. Possible failure following promise must be provided for. Never must I feel myself called upon to do this kind of thing again. Besides, I have never got over the Zabriskie tragedy. It haunts me continually. Something new may help to put it out of my head. I feel guilty. I was responsible — "

"No, Puss. I will not have it that you were responsible. Some such end was bound to follow a complication like that. Sooner or later he would have been driven to shoot himself — "

"But not her."

"No, not her. But do you think she would have given those few minutes of perfect understanding with her blind husband for a few years more of miserable life?"

Violet made no answer; she was too absorbed in her surprise. Was this Arthur? Had a few weeks' work and a close connection with the really serious things of life made this change in him? Her face beamed at the thought, which seeing, but not understanding what underlay this evidence of joy, he bent and kissed her, saying with some of his old nonchalance:

"Forget it, Violet; only don't let anyone or anything lead you to interest yourself in another affair of the kind. If you do, I shall have to consult a certain friend of yours as to the best way of stopping this folly. I mention no names. Oh! you need not look so frightened. Only behave; that's all."

"He's right," she acknowledged to herself, as he sauntered away; "altogether right."

Yet because she wanted the extra money —

*****

The scene invited alarm, — that is, for so young a girl as Violet, surveying it from an automobile some time after the stroke of midnight. An unknown house at the end of a heavily shaded walk, in the open doorway of which could be seen the silhouette of a woman's form leaning eagerly forward with arms outstretched in an appeal for help! It vanished while she looked, but the effect remained, holding her to her seat for one startled moment. This seemed strange, for she had anticipated adventure. One is not summoned from a private ball to ride a dozen miles into the country on an errand of investigation, without some expectation of encountering the mysterious and the tragic. But Violet Strange, for all her many experiences, was of a most susceptible nature, and for the instant in which that door stood open, with only the memory of that expectant figure to disturb the faintly lit vista of the hall beyond, she felt that grip upon the throat which comes from an indefinable fear which no words can explain and no plummet sound.

But this soon passed. With the setting of her foot to ground, conditions changed and her emotions took on a more normal character. The figure of a man now stood in the place held by the vanished woman, and it was not only that of one she knew but that of one whom she trusted — a friend whose very presence gave her courage. With this recognition came a better understanding of the situation, and it was with a beaming eye and unclouded features that she tripped up the walk to meet the expectant figure and outstretched hand of Roger Upjohn.

"You here!" she exclaimed, amid smiles and blushes, as he drew her into the hall.

He at once launched forth into explanations mingled with apologies for the presumption he had shown in putting her to this inconvenience. There was trouble in the house — great trouble. Something had occurred for which an explanation must be found before morning, or the happiness and honour of more than one person now under this unhappy roof would be wrecked. He knew it was late — that she had been obliged to take a long and dreary ride alone, but her success with the problem which had once come near wrecking his own life had emboldened him to telephone to the office and — "But you are in ball-dress," he cried in amazement. "Did you think — "

"I came from a ball. Word reached me between the dances. I did not go home. I had been bidden to hurry."

He looked his appreciation, but when he spoke it was to say:

"This is the situation. Miss Digby — "

"The lady who is to be married to-morrow?"

"Who *hopes* to be married to-morrow."

"How, *hopes*?"

"Who *will* be married to-morrow, if a certain article lost in this house to-night can be found before any of the persons who have been dining here leave for their homes."

Violet uttered an exclamation.

"Then, Mr. Cornell — " she began.

"Mr. Cornell has our utmost confidence," Roger hastened to interpose. "But the article missing is one which he might reasonably desire to possess and which he alone of all present had the opportunity of securing. You can therefore see why he, with his pride — the pride of a man not rich, engaged to marry a woman who is — should declare that unless his innocence is established before daybreak, the doors of St. Bartholomew will remain shut to-morrow."

"But the article lost — what is it?"

"Miss Digby will give you the particulars. She is waiting to receive you," he added with a gesture towards a half-open door at their right.

Violet glanced that way, then cast her looks up and down the hall in which they stood.

"Do you know that you have not told me in whose house I am? Not hers, I know. She lives in the city."

"And you are twelve miles from Harlem. Miss Strange, you are in the Van Broecklyn mansion, famous enough you will acknowledge. Have you never been here before?"

"I have been by here, but I recognized nothing in the dark. What an exciting place for an investigation!"

"And Mr. Van Broecklyn? Have you never met him?"

"Once, when a child. He frightened me *then*."

"And may frighten you now; though I doubt it. Time has mellowed him. Besides, I have prepared him for what might otherwise occasion him some astonishment. Naturally he would not look for just the sort of lady investigator I am about to introduce to him."

She smiled. Violet Strange was a very charming young woman, as well as a keen prober of odd mysteries.

The meeting between herself and Miss Digby was a sympathetic one. After the first inevitable shock which the latter felt at sight of the beauty and fashionable appearance of the mysterious little being who was to solve her difficulties, her glance, which under other circumstances might have lingered unduly upon the piquant features and exquisite dressing of the fairy-like figure before her, passed at once to Violet's eyes in whose steady depths beamed an intelligence quite at odds with the coquettish dimples which so often misled the casual observer in his estimation of a character singularly subtle and well-poised.

As for the impression she herself made upon

Violet — it was the same she made upon everyone. No one could look long at Florence Digby and not recognize the loftiness of her spirit and the generous nature of her impulses. In person she was tall, and as she leaned to take Violet's hand, the difference between them brought out the salient points in each, to the great admiration of the one onlooker.

Meantime for all her interest in the case in hand, Violet could not help casting a hurried look about her, in gratification of the curiosity incited by her entrance into a house signalized from its foundation by such a series of tragic events. The result was disappointing. The walls were plain, the furniture simple. Nothing suggestive in either, unless it was the fact that nothing was new, nothing modern. As it looked in the days of Burr and Hamilton so it looked to-day, even to the rather startling detail of candles which did duty on every side in place of gas.

As Violet recalled the reason for this the fascination of the past seized upon her imagination. There was no knowing where this might have carried her, had not the feverish gleam in Miss Digby's eyes warned her that the present held its own excitement. Instantly, she was all attention and listening with undivided mind to that lady's disclosures.

They were brief and to the following effect:

The dinner which had brought some half-dozen people together in this house had been given in celebration of her impending marriage. But it was also in a way meant as a compliment to one of the other guests, a Mr. Spielhagen, who, during the week, had succeeded in demonstrating to a few experts the value of a discovery he had made which would transform a great industry.

In speaking of this discovery, Miss Digby did not go into particulars, the whole matter being far beyond her understanding; but in stating its value she openly acknowledged that it was in the line of Mr. Cornell's own work, and one which involved calculations and a formula which, if prematurely disclosed, would invalidate the contract Mr. Spielhagen hoped to make, and thus destroy his present hopes.

Of this formula but two copies existed. One was locked up in a safe-deposit vault in Boston, the other he had brought into the house on his person, and it was the latter which was now missing, it having been abstracted during the evening from a manuscript of sixteen or more sheets, under circumstances which he would now endeavour to relate.

Mr. Van Broecklyn, their host, had in his melancholy life but one interest which could be called at all absorbing. This was for explosives. As a consequence, much of the talk at the dinner-table had been on Mr. Spielhagen's discovery, and the possible changes it might introduce into this especial industry. As these, worked out from a formula kept secret from the trade, could not but affect greatly Mr. Cornell's interests, she found herself listening intently, when Mr. Van Broecklyn, with an apology for his interference, ventured to remark that if Mr. Spielhagen had made a valuable discovery in this line, so had he, and one which he had substantiated by many experiments. It was not a marketable one, such as Mr. Spielhagen's was, but in his work upon the same, and in the tests which he had been led to make, he had discovered certain instances he would gladly name, which demanded exceptional procedure to be successful. If Mr. Spielhagen's method did not allow for these exceptions, nor make suitable provision for them, then Mr. Spielhagen's method would fail more times than it would succeed. Did it so allow and so provide? It would relieve him greatly to learn that it did.

The answer came quickly. Yes, it did. But later and after some further conversation, Mr. Spielhagen's confidence seemed to wane, and before they left the dinner-table, he openly declared his intention of looking over his manuscript again that very night, in order to be sure that the formula therein contained duly covered all the exceptions mentioned by Mr. Van Broecklyn.

If Mr. Cornell's countenance showed any change at this moment, she for one had not noticed it; but the bitterness with which he remarked upon the other's good fortune in having discovered this formula of whose entire success he had no doubt, was apparent to everybody, and naturally gave point to the circumstances which a short time afterward associated him with the disappearance of the same.

The ladies (there were two others besides herself) having withdrawn in a body to the music-room, the gentlemen all proceeded to the library to smoke. Here, conversation loosed from the one topic which had hitherto engrossed it, was proceeding briskly, when Mr. Spielhagen, with a nervous gesture, impulsively looked about him and said:

"I cannot rest till I have run through my thesis again. Where can I find a quiet spot? I won't be long; I read very rapidly."

It was for Mr. Van Broecklyn to answer, but no word coming from him, every eye turned his way, only to find him sunk in one of those fits of abstraction so well known to his friends, and from which no one who has this strange man's peace of mind at heart ever presumes to rouse him.

What was to be done? These moods of their singular host sometimes lasted half an hour, and Mr. Spielhagen had not the appearance of a man of patience. Indeed he presently gave proof of the great uneasiness he was labouring under, for noticing a door standing ajar on the other side of the room, he remarked to those around him:

"A den! and lighted! Do you see any objection to my shutting myself in there for a few minutes?"

No one venturing to reply, he rose, and giving a slight push to the door, disclosed a small room exquisitely panelled and brightly lighted, but without one article of furniture in it, not even a chair.

"The very place," quoth Mr. Spielhagen, and lifting a light cane-bottomed chair from the many standing about, he carried it inside and shut the door behind him.

Several minutes passed during which the man who had served at table entered with a tray on which were several small glasses evidently containing some choice liqueur. Finding his master fixed in one of his strange moods, he set the tray down and, pointing to one of the glasses, said:

"That is for Mr. Van Broecklyn. It contains his usual quieting powder." And urging the gentlemen to help themselves, he quietly left the room.

Mr. Upjohn lifted the glass nearest him, and Mr. Cornell seemed about to do the same when he suddenly reached forward and catching up one farther off started for the room in which Mr. Spielhagen had so deliberately secluded himself.

Why he did all this — why, above all things, he should reach across the tray for a glass instead of taking the one under his hand, he can no more explain than why he has followed many another unhappy impulse. Nor did he understand the nervous start given by Mr. Spielhagen at his entrance, or the stare with which that gentleman took the glass from his hand and mechanically drank its contents, till he saw how his hand had stretched itself across the sheet of paper he was reading, in an open attempt to hide the lines visible between his fingers. Then indeed the intruder flushed and withdrew in great embarrassment, fully conscious of his indiscretion but not deeply disturbed till Mr. Van Broecklyn, suddenly arousing and glancing down at the tray placed very near his hand, remarked in some surprise: "Dobbs seems to have forgotten me." Then indeed, the unfortunate Mr. Cornell realized what he had done. It was the glass intended for his host which he had caught up and carried into the other room — the glass which he had been told contained a drug. Of what folly he had been guilty, and how tame would be any effort at excuse!

Attempting none, he rose and with a hurried glance at Mr. Upjohn who flushed in sympathy at his distress, he crossed to the door he had so lately closed upon Mr. Spielhagen. But feeling his shoulder touched as his hand pressed the knob, he turned to meet the eye of Mr. Van Broecklyn fixed upon him with an expression which utterly confounded him.

"Where are you going?" that gentleman asked.

The questioning tone, the severe look, expressive at once of displeasure and astonishment, were most disconcerting, but Mr. Cornell managed to stammer forth:

"Mr. Spielhagen is in here consulting his thesis. When your man brought in the cordial, I was awkward enough to catch up your glass and carry it in to Mr. Spielhagen. He drank it and I — I am anxious to see if it did him any harm."

As he uttered the last word he felt Mr. Van Broecklyn's hand slip from his shoulder, but no word accompanied the action, nor did his host make the least move to follow him into the room.

This was a matter of great regret to him later, as it left him for a moment out of the range of every eye, during which he says he simply stood in a state of shock at seeing Mr. Spielhagen still sitting there, manuscript in hand, but with head fallen forward and eyes closed; dead, asleep or — he hardly knew what; the sight so paralyzed him.

Whether or not this was the exact truth and the whole truth, Mr. Cornell certainly looked very unlike himself as he stepped back into Mr. Van Broecklyn's presence; and he was only partially reassured when that gentleman protested that there was no real harm in the drug, and that Mr. Spielhagen would be all right if left to wake naturally and without shock. However, as his present attitude was one of great discomfort, they decided to carry him back and lay him on the library lounge. But before doing this, Mr. Upjohn drew from his flaccid grasp the precious manuscript, and carrying it into the larger room placed it on a remote table, where it remained undisturbed till Mr. Spielhagen, suddenly coming to himself at the end of some fifteen minutes, missed the sheets from his hand, and bounding up, crossed the room to repossess himself of them.

His face, as he lifted them up and rapidly ran through them with ever-accumulating anxiety, told them what they had to expect.

The page containing the formula was gone!

*****

Violet now saw her problem.

II

There was no doubt about the loss I have mentioned; all could see that page 13 was not there. In vain a second handling of every sheet, the one so numbered was not to be found. Page 14 met the eye on the top of the pile, and page 12 finished it off at the bottom, but no page 13 in between, or anywhere else.

Where had it vanished, and through whose agency had this misadventure occurred? No one could say, or, at least, no one there made any attempt to do so, though everybody started to look for it.

But where look? The adjoining small room offered no facilities for hiding a cigar-end, much less a square of shining white paper. Bare walls, a bare floor, and a single chair for furniture, comprised all that was to be seen in this direction. Nor could the room in which they then stood be thought to hold it, unless it was on the person of some one of them. Could this be the explanation of the mystery? No man looked his doubts; but Mr. Cornell, possibly divining the general feeling, stepped up to Mr. Van Broecklyn and in a cool voice, but with the red burning hotly on either cheek, said so as to be heard by everyone present:

"I demand to be searched — at once and thoroughly."

A moment's silence, then the common cry:

"We will all be searched."

"Is Mr. Spielhagen sure that the missing page was with the others when he sat down in the adjoining room to read his thesis?" asked their perturbed host.

"Very sure," came the emphatic reply. "Indeed, I was just going through the formula itself when I fell asleep."

"You are ready to assert this?"

"I am ready to swear it."

Mr. Cornell repeated his request.

"I demand that you make a thorough search of my person. I must be cleared, and instantly, of every suspicion," he gravely asserted, "or how can I marry Miss Digby to-morrow?"

After that there was no further hesitation. One and all subjected themselves to the ordeal suggested; even Mr. Spielhagen. But this effort was as futile as the rest. The lost page was not found.

What were they to think? What were they to do?

There seemed to be nothing left to do, and yet some further attempt must be made towards the recovery of this important formula. Mr. Cornell's marriage and Mr. Spielhagen's business success both depended upon its being in the latter's hands before six in the morning, when he was engaged to hand it over again to a certain manufacturer sailing for Europe on an early steamer.

Five hours!

Had Mr. Van Broecklyn a suggestion to offer? No, he was as much at sea as the rest.

Simultaneously look crossed look. Blankness was on every face.

"Let us call the ladies," suggested one.

It was done, and however great the tension had been before, it was even greater when Miss Digby stepped upon the scene. But she was not a woman to be shaken from her poise even by a crisis of this importance. When the dilemma had been presented to her and the full situation grasped, she looked first at Mr. Cornell and then at Mr. Spielhagen, and quietly said:

"There is but one explanation possible of this matter. Mr. Spielhagen will excuse me, but he is evidently mistaken in thinking that he saw the lost page among the rest. The condition into which he was thrown by the unaccustomed drug he had drank, made him liable to hallucinations. I have not the least doubt he thought he had been studying the formula at the time he dropped off to sleep. I have every confidence in the gentleman's candour. But so have I in that of Mr. Cornell," she supplemented, with a smile.

An exclamation from Mr. Van Broecklyn and a subdued murmur from all but Mr. Spielhagen testified to the effect of this suggestion, and there is no saying what might have been the result if Mr. Cornell had not hurriedly put in this extraordinary and most unexpected protest:

"Miss Digby has my gratitude," said he, "for a confidence which I hope to prove to be deserved. But I must say this for Mr. Spielhagen. He was correct in stating that he was engaged in looking over his formula when I stepped into his presence with the glass of cordial. If you were not in a position to see the hurried way in which his hand instinctively spread itself over the page he was reading, I was; and if that does not seem conclusive to you, then I feel bound to state that in unconsciously following this movement of his, I plainly saw the number written on the top of the page, and that number was — 13."

A loud exclamation, this time from Spielhagen himself, announced his gratitude and corresponding change of attitude toward the speaker.

"Wherever that damned page has gone," he protested, advancing towards Cornell with outstretched hand, "you have nothing to do with its disappearance."

Instantly all constraint fled, and every countenance took on a relieved expression. *But the problem remained.*

Suddenly those very words passed someone's lips, and with their utterance Mr. Upjohn remembered how at an extraordinary crisis in his own life, he had been helped and an equally difficult problem settled, by a little lady secretly attached to a private detective agency. If she could only be found and hurried here before morning, all might yet be well. He would make the effort. Such wild schemes sometimes work. He telephoned to the office and —

Was there anything else Miss Strange would like to know?

III

Miss Strange, thus appealed to, asked where the gentlemen were now.

She was told that they were still all together in the library; the ladies had been sent home.

"Then let us go to them," said Violet, hiding under a smile her great fear that here was an affair which might very easily spell for her that dismal word, *failure*.

So great was that fear that under all ordinary circumstances she would have had no thought for anything else in the short interim between this stating of the problem and her speedy entrance among the persons involved. But the circumstances of this case were so far from ordinary, or rather let me put it in this way, the setting of the case was so very extraordinary, that she scarcely thought of the problem before her, in her great interest in the house through whose rambling halls she was being so carefully guided. So much that was tragic and heart-rending had occurred here. The Van Broecklyn name, the Van Broecklyn history, above all the Van Broecklyn tradition, which made the house unique in the country's annals, all made an appeal to her imagination, and centred her thoughts on what she saw about her. There was a door which no man ever opened — had never opened since Revolutionary times — should she see it? Should she know it if she did see it? Then Mr. Van Broecklyn himself! Just to meet him, under any conditions and in any place, was an event. But to meet him here, under the pall of his own mystery! No wonder she had no words for her companions, or that her thoughts clung to this anticipation in wonder and almost fearsome delight.

His story was a well-known one. A bachelor and a misanthrope, he lived absolutely alone save for a large entourage of servants, all men and elderly ones at that. He never visited. Though he now and then, as on this occasion, entertained certain persons under his roof, he declined every invitation for himself, avoiding even, with equal strictness, all evening amusements of whatever kind, which would detain him in the city after ten at night. Perhaps this was to ensure no break in his rule of life never to sleep out of his own bed. Though he was a man well over fifty he had not spent, according to his own statement, but two nights out of his own bed since his return from Europe in early boyhood, and those were in obedience to a judicial summons which took him to Boston.

This was his main eccentricity, but he had another which is apparent enough from what has already been said. He avoided women. If thrown in with them during his short visits into town, he was invariably polite and at all times companionable, but he never sought them out, nor had gossip, contrary to its usual habit, ever linked his name with one of the sex.

Yet he was a man of more than ordinary attraction. His features were fine and his figure impressive. He might have been the cynosure of all eyes had he chosen to enter crowded drawing-rooms, or even to frequent public assemblages, but having turned his back upon everything of the kind in his youth, he had found it impossible to alter his habits with advancing years; nor was he now expected to. The position he had taken was respected. Leonard Van Broecklyn was no longer criticized.

Was there any explanation for this strangely

self-centred life? Those who knew him best seemed to think so. In the first place he had sprung from an unfortunate stock. Events of an unusual and tragic nature had marked the family of both parents. Nor had his parents themselves been exempt from this seeming fatality. Antagonistic in tastes and temperament, they had dragged on an unhappy existence in the old home, till both natures rebelled, and a separation ensued which not only disunited their lives but sent them to opposite sides of the globe never to return again. At least, that was the inference drawn from the peculiar circumstances attending the event. On the morning of one never-to-be-forgotten day, John Van Broecklyn, the grandfather of the present representative of the family, found the following note from his son lying on the library table:

"Father:

"Life in this house, or any house, with *her* is no longer endurable. One of us must go. The mother should not be separated from her child. Therefore it is I whom you will never see again. Forget me, but be considerate of her and the boy.

"William."

Six hours later another note was found, this time; from the wife:

"Father:

"Tied to a rotting corpse what does one do? Lop off one's arm if necessary to rid one of the contact. As all love between your son and myself is dead, I can no longer live within the sound of his voice. As this is his home, he is the one to remain in it. May our child reap the benefit of his mother's loss and his father's affection.

"Rhoda."

Both were gone, and gone forever. Simultaneous in their departure, they preserved each his own silence and sent no word back. If the one went East and the other West, they may have met on the other side of the globe, but never again in the home which sheltered their boy. For him and for his grandfather they had sunk from sight in the great sea of humanity, leaving them stranded on an isolated and mournful shore. The grandfather steeled himself to the double loss, for the child's sake; but the boy of eleven succumbed. Few of the world's great sufferers, of whatever age or condition, have mourned as this child mourned, or shown the effects of his grief so deeply or so long. Not till he had passed his majority did the line, carved in one day in his baby forehead, lose any of its intensity; and there are those who declare that even later than that, the midnight stillness of the house was disturbed from time to time by his muffled shriek of "Mother! Mother!" sending the servants from the house, and adding one more horror to the many which clung about this accursed mansion.

Of this cry Violet had heard, and it was that and the door — But I have already told you about the door which she was still looking for, when her two companions suddenly halted, and she found herself on the threshold of the library, in full view of Mr. Van Broecklyn and his two guests.

Slight and fairy-like in figure, with an air of modest reserve more in keeping with her youth and dainty dimpling beauty than with her errand, her appearance produced an astonishment which none of the gentlemen were able to disguise. This the clever detective, with a genius for social problems and odd elusive cases! This darling of the ball-room in satin and pearls! Mr. Spielhagen glanced at Mr. Carroll, and Mr. Carroll at Mr. Spielhagen, and both at Mr. Upjohn, in very evident distrust. As for Violet, she had eyes only for Mr. Van Broecklyn who stood before her in a surprise equal to that of the others but with more restraint in its expression.

She was not disappointed in him. She had expected to see a man, reserved almost to the point of austerity. And she found his first look even more awe-compelling than her imagination had pictured; so much so indeed, that her resolution faltered, and she took a quick step backward; which seeing, he smiled and her heart and hopes grew warm again. That he could smile, and smile with absolute sweetness, was her great comfort when later — But I am introducing you too hurriedly to the catastrophe. There is much to be told first.

I pass over the preliminaries, and come at once to the moment when Violet, having listened to a repetition of the full facts, stood with downcast eyes before these gentlemen, complaining in some alarm to herself:

"They expect me to tell them now and without further search or parley just where this missing page is. I shall have to balk that expectation without losing their confidence. But how?"

Summoning up her courage and meeting each inquiring eye with a look which seemed to carry a different message to each, she remarked very quietly:

"This is not a matter to guess at. I must have time and I must look a little deeper into the facts just given me. I presume that the table I see over there is the one upon which Mr. Upjohn laid the manuscript during Mr. Spielhagen's unconsciousness."

All nodded.

"Is it — I mean the table — in the same condition it was then? Has nothing been taken from it except the manuscript?"

"Nothing."

"Then the missing page is not there," she smiled, pointing to its bare top. A pause, during which she stood with her gaze fixed on the floor before her. She was thinking and thinking hard.

Suddenly she came to a decision. Addressing Mr. Upjohn she asked if he were quite sure that in taking the manuscript from Mr. Spielhagen's hand he had neither disarranged nor dropped one of its pages.

The answer was unequivocal.

"Then," she declared, with quiet assurance and a steady meeting with her own of every eye, "as the thirteenth page was not found among the others when they were taken from this table, nor on the persons of either Mr. Carroll or Mr. Spielhagen, it is still in that inner room."

"Impossible!" came from every lip, each in a different tone. "That room is absolutely empty."

"May I have a look at its emptiness?" she asked, with a naïve glance at Mr. Van Broecklyn.

"There is positively nothing in the room but the chair Mr. Spielhagen sat on," objected that gentleman with a noticeable air of reluctance.

"Still, may I not have a look at it?" she persisted, with that disarming smile she kept for great occasions.

Mr. Van Broecklyn bowed. He could not refuse a request so urged, but his step was slow and his manner next to ungracious as he led the way to the door of the adjoining room and threw it open.

Just what she had been told to expect! Bare walls and floors and an empty chair! Yet she did not instantly withdraw, but stood silently contemplating the panelled wainscoting surrounding her, as though she suspected it of containing some secret hiding-place not apparent to the eye.

Mr. Van Broecklyn, noting this, hastened to say:

"The walls are sound, Miss Strange. They contain no hidden cupboards."

"And that door?" she asked, pointing to a portion of the wainscoting so exactly like the rest that only the most experienced eye could detect the line of deeper colour which marked an opening.

For an instant Mr. Van Broecklyn stood rigid, then the immovable pallor, which was one of his chief characteristics, gave way to a deep flush, as he explained:

"There was a door there once; but it has been permanently closed. With cement," he forced himself to add, his countenance losing its evanescent colour till it shone ghastly again in the strong light.

With difficulty Violet preserved her show of composure. "*The* door!" she murmured to herself. "I have found it. The great historic door!" But her tone was light as she ventured to say:

"Then it can no longer be opened by your hand or any other?"

"It could not be opened with an axe."

Violet sighed in the midst of her triumph. Her curiosity had been satisfied, but the problem she had been set to solve looked inexplicable. But she was not one to yield easily to discouragement. Marking the disappointment approaching to disdain in every eye but Mr. Upjohn's, she drew herself up — (she had not far to draw) and made this final proposal.

"A sheet of paper," she remarked, "of the size of this one cannot be spirited away, or dissolved into thin air. It exists; it is here; and all we want is some happy thought in order to find it. I acknowledge that that happy thought has not come to me yet, but sometimes I get it in what may seem to you a very odd way. Forgetting myself, I try to assume the individuality of the person who has worked the mystery. If I can think with his thoughts, I possibly may follow him in his actions. In this case I should like to make believe for a few moments that I am Mr. Spielhagen" (with what a delicious smile she said this). "I should like to hold his thesis in my hand and be interrupted in my reading by Mr. Cornell offering his glass of cordial; then I should like to nod and slip off mentally into a deep sleep. Possibly in that sleep the dream may come which will clarify the whole situation. Will you humour me so far?"

A ridiculous concession, but finally she had her way; the farce was enacted and they left her as she had requested them to do, alone with her dreams in the small room.

Suddenly they heard her cry out, and in another moment she appeared before them, the picture of excitement.

"Is this chair standing exactly as it did when Mr. Spielhagen occupied it?" she asked.

"No," said Mr. Upjohn, "it faced the other way."

She stepped back and twirled the chair about with her disengaged hand.

"So?"

Mr. Upjohn and Mr. Spielhagen both nodded, so did the others when she glanced at them.

With a sign of ill-concealed satisfaction, she drew their attention to herself; then eagerly cried:

"Gentlemen, look here!"

Seating herself, she allowed her whole body to relax till she presented the picture of one calmly asleep. Then, as they continued to gaze at her with fascinated eyes, not knowing what to expect, they saw something white escape from her lap and slide across the floor till it touched and was stayed by the wainscot. It was the top page of the manuscript she held, and as some inkling of the truth reached their astonished minds, she sprang impetuously to her feet and, pointing to the fallen sheet, cried:

"Do you understand now? Look where it lies, and then look here!"

She had bounded toward the wall and was now on her knees pointing to the bottom of the wainscot, just a few inches to the left of the fallen page.

"A crack!" she cried, "under what was once the door. It's a very thin one, hardly perceptible to the eye. But see!" Here she laid her finger on the fallen paper and drawing it towards her, pushed it carefully against the lower edge of the wainscot. Half of it at once disappeared.

"I could easily slip it all through," she assured them, withdrawing the sheet and leaping to her feet in triumph. "You know now where the missing page lies, Mr. Spielhagen. All that remains is for Mr. Van Broecklyn to get it for you."

IV

The cries of mingled astonishment and relief which greeted this simple elucidation of the mystery were broken by a curiously choked, almost unintelligible, cry. It came from the man thus appealed to, who, unnoticed by them all, had started at her first word and gradually, as action followed action, withdrawn himself till he now stood alone and in an attitude almost of defiance behind the large table in the centre of the library.

"I am sorry," he began, with a brusqueness which gradually toned down into a forced urbanity as he beheld every eye fixed upon him in amazement, "that circumstances forbid my being of assistance to you in this unfortunate matter. If the paper lies where you say, and I see no other explanation of its loss, I am afraid it will have to remain there for this night at least. The cement in which that door is embedded is thick as any wall; it would take men with pickaxes, possibly with dynamite, to make a breach there wide enough for anyone to reach in. And we are far from any such help."

In the midst of the consternation caused by

these words, the clock on the mantel behind his back rang out the hour. It was but a double stroke, but that meant two hours after midnight and had the effect of a knell in the hearts of those most interested.

"But I am expected to give that formula into the hands of our manager before six o'clock in the morning. The steamer sails at a quarter after."

"Can't you reproduce a copy of it from memory?" someone asked; "and insert it in its proper place among the pages you hold there?"

"The paper would not be the same. That would lead to questions and the truth would come out. As the chief value of the process contained in that formula lies in its secrecy, no explanation I could give would relieve me from the suspicions which an acknowledgment of the existence of a third copy, however well hidden, would entail. I should lose my great opportunity."

Mr. Cornell's state of mind can be imagined. In an access of mingled regret and despair, he cast a glance at Violet, who, with a nod of understanding, left the little room in which they still stood, and approached Mr. Van Broecklyn.

Lifting up her head, — for he was very tall, — and instinctively rising on her toes the nearer to reach his ear, she asked in a cautious whisper:

"Is there no other way of reaching that place?"

She acknowledged afterwards, that for one moment her heart stood still from fear, such a change took place in his face, though she says he did not move a muscle. Then, just when she was expecting from him some harsh or forbidding word, he wheeled abruptly away from her and crossing to a window at his side, lifted the shade and looked out. When he returned, he was his usual self so far as she could see.

"There is a way," he now confided to her in a tone as low as her own, "but it can only be taken by a child."

"Not by me?" she asked, smiling down at her own childish proportions.

For an instant he seemed taken aback, then she saw his hand begin to tremble and his lips twitch. Somehow — she knew not why — she began to pity him, and asked herself as she felt rather than saw the struggle in his mind, that here was a trouble which if once understood would greatly dwarf that of the two men in the room behind them.

"I am discreet," she whisperingly declared. "I have heard the history of that door — how it was against the tradition of the family to have it opened. There must have been some very dreadful reason. But old superstitions do not affect me, and if you will allow me to take the way you mention, I will follow your bidding exactly, and will not trouble myself about anything but the recovery of this paper, which must lie only a little way inside that blocked-up door."

Was his look one of rebuke at her presumption, or just the constrained expression of a perturbed mind? Probably, the latter, for while she watched him for some understanding of his mood, he reached out his hand and touched one of the satin folds crossing her shoulder.

"You would soil this irretrievably," said he.

"There is stuff in the stores for another," she smiled. Slowly his touch deepened into pressure. Watching him she saw the crust of some old fear or dominant superstition melt under her eyes, and was quite prepared, when he remarked, with what for him was a lightsome air:

"I will buy the stuff, if you will dare the darkness and intricacies of our old cellar. I can give you no light. You will have to feel your way according to my direction."

"I am ready to dare anything."

He left her abruptly.

"I will warn Miss Digby," he called back. "She shall go with you as far as the cellar."

V

Violet in her short career as an investigator of mysteries had been in many a situation calling for more than womanly nerve and courage. But never — or so it seemed to her at the time — had she experienced a greater depression of spirit than when she stood with Miss Digby before a small door at the extreme end of the cellar, and understood that here was her road — a road which once entered, she must take alone.

First, it was such a small door! No child older than eleven could possibly squeeze through it. But she was of the size of a child of eleven and might possibly manage that difficulty.

Secondly: there are always some unforeseen possibilities in every situation, and though she had listened carefully to Mr. Van Broecklyn's directions and was sure that she knew them by heart, she wished she had kissed her father more tenderly in leaving him that night for the ball, and that she had not pouted so undutifully at some harsh stricture he had made. Did this mean fear? She despised the feeling if it did.

Thirdly: She hated darkness. She knew this when she offered herself for this undertaking; but she was in a bright room at the moment and only imagined what she must now face as a reality. But one jet had been lit in the cellar and that near the entrance. Mr. Van Broecklyn seemed not to need light, even in his unfastening of the small door which Violet was sure had been protected by more than one lock.

Doubt, shadow, and a solitary climb between unknown walls, with only a streak of light for her goal, and the clinging pressure of Florence Digby's hand on her own for solace — surely the prospect was one to tax the courage of her young heart to its limit. But she had promised, and she would fulfil. So with a brave smile she stooped to the little door, and in another moment had started on her journey.

For journey the shortest distance may seem when every inch means a heart-throb and one grows old in traversing a foot. At first the way was easy; she had but to crawl up a slight incline with the comforting consciousness that two people were within reach of her voice, almost within sound of her beating heart. But presently she came to a turn, beyond which her fingers failed to reach any wall on her left. Then came a step up which she stumbled, and farther on a short flight, each tread of which she had been told to test before she ventured to climb it, lest the decay of innumerable years should have weakened the wood too much to bear her weight. One, two, three, four, five steps! Then a landing with an open space beyond. Half of her journey was done. Here she felt she could give a minute to drawing her breath naturally, if the air, unchanged in years, would allow her to do so. Besides, here she had been enjoined to do a certain thing and to do it according to instructions. Three matches had been given her and a little night candle. Denied all light up to now, it was at this point she was to light her candle and place it on the floor, so that in returning she should not miss the staircase and get a fall. She had promised to do this, and was only too happy to see a spark of light scintillate into life in the immeasurable darkness.

She was now in a great room long closed to the world, where once officers in Colonial wars had feasted, and more than one council had been held. A room, too, which had seen more than one tragic happening, as its almost unparalleled isolation proclaimed. So much Mr. Van Broecklyn had told her, but she was warned to be careful in traversing it and not upon any pretext to swerve aside from the right-hand wall till she came to a huge mantelpiece. This passed, and a sharp corner turned, she ought to see somewhere in the dim spaces before her a streak of vivid light shining through the crack at the bottom of the blocked-up door. The paper should be somewhere near this streak.

All simple, all easy of accomplishment, if only that streak of light were all she was likely to see or think of. If the horror which was gripping her throat should not take shape! If things would remain shrouded in impenetrable darkness, and not force themselves in shadowy suggestion upon her excited fancy! But the blackness of the passageway through which she had just struggled, was not to be found here. Whether it was the effect of that small flame flickering at the top of the staircase behind her, or of some change in her own powers of seeing, surely there was a difference in her present outlook. Tall shapes were becoming visible — the air was no longer blank — she could see — Then suddenly she saw why. In the wall high up on her right was a window. It was small and all but invisible, being covered on the outside with vines, and on the inside with the cobwebs of a century. But some small gleams from the starlight night came through, making phantasms out of ordinary things, which unseen were horrible enough, and half seen choked her heart with terror.

"I cannot bear it," she whispered to herself even while creeping forward, her hand upon the wall. "I will close my eyes" was her next thought. "I will make my own darkness," and with a spasmodic forcing of her lids together, she continued to creep on, passing the mantelpiece, where she knocked against something which fell with an awful clatter.

This sound, followed as it was by that of smothered voices from the excited group awaiting the result of her experiment from behind the impenetrable wall she should be nearing now if she had followed her instructions aright, freed her instantly from her fancies; and opening her eyes once more, she cast a look ahead, and to her delight, saw but a few steps away, the thin streak of bright light which marked the end of her journey.

It took her but a moment after that to find the missing page, and picking it up in haste from the dusty floor, she turned herself quickly about and joyfully began to retrace her steps. Why, then, was it that in the course of a few minutes more her voice suddenly broke into a wild, unearthly shriek, which ringing with terror burst the bounds of that dungeon-like room, and sank, a barbed shaft, into the breasts of those awaiting the result of her doubtful adventure, at either end of this dread nothoroughfare.

What had happened?

If they had thought to look out, they would have seen that the moon — held in check by a bank of cloud occupying half the heavens — had suddenly burst its bounds and was sending long bars of revealing light into every uncurtained window.

VI

Florence Digby, in her short and sheltered life, had possibly never known any very great or deep emotion. But she touched the bottom of extreme terror at that moment, as with her ears still thrilling with Violet's piercing cry, she turned to look at Mr. Van Broecklyn, and beheld the instantaneous wreck it had made of this seemingly strong man. Not till he came to lie in his coffin would he show a more ghastly countenance; and trembling herself almost to the point of falling, she caught him by the arm and sought to read in his face what had happened. Something disastrous she was sure; something which he had feared and was partially prepared for, yet which in happening had crushed him. Was it a pitfall into which the poor little lady had fallen? If so — But he is speaking — mumbling low words to himself. Some of them she can hear. He is reproaching himself — repeating over and over that he should never have taken such a chance; that he should have remembered her youth — the weakness of a young girl's nerve. He had been mad, and now — and now —

With the repetition of this word his murmuring ceased. All his energies were now absorbed in listening at the low door separating him from what he was agonizing to know — a door impossible to enter, impossible to enlarge — a barrier to all help — an opening whereby sound might pass but nothing else save her own small body, now lying — where?

"Is she hurt?" faltered Florence, stooping, herself, to listen. "Can you hear anything — anything?"

For an instant he did not answer; every faculty was absorbed in the one sense; then slowly and in gasps he began to mutter:

"I think — I hear — *something*. Her step — no, no, no step. All is as quiet as death; not a sound, — not a breath — she has fainted. O God! O God! Why this calamity on top of all!"

He had sprung to his feet at the utterance of this invocation, but next moment was down on his knees again, listening — listening.

Never was silence more profound; they were hearkening for murmurs from a tomb. Florence began to sense the full horror of it all, and was swaying helplessly when Mr. Van Broecklyn impulsively lifted his hand in an admonitory Hush! and through the daze of her faculties a small far sound began to make itself heard, growing louder as she waited, then becoming faint again, then altogether ceasing only to renew itself once more, till it resolved into an approaching step, faltering in its course, but coming ever nearer and nearer.

"She's safe! She's not hurt!" sprang from Florence's lips in inexpressible relief; and expecting Mr.

Van Broecklyn to show an equal joy, she turned toward him, with the cheerful cry.

"Now if she has been so fortunate as to find that missing page, we shall all be repaid for our fright."

A movement on his part, a shifting of position which brought him finally to his feet, but he gave no other proof of having heard her, nor did his countenance mirror her relief. "It is as if he dreaded, instead of hailed, her return," was Florence's inward comment as she watched him involuntarily recoil at each fresh token of Violet's advance.

Yet because this seemed so very unnatural, she persisted in her efforts to lighten the situation, and when he made no attempt to encourage Violet in her approach, she herself stooped and called out a cheerful welcome which must have rung sweetly in the poor little detective's ears.

A sorry sight was Violet, when, helped by Florence she finally crawled into view through the narrow opening and stood once again on the cellar floor. Pale, trembling, and soiled with the dust of years, she presented a helpless figure enough, till the joy in Florence's face recalled some of her spirit, and, glancing down at her hand in which a sheet of paper was visible, she asked for Mr. Spielhagen.

"I've got the formula," she said. "If you will bring him, I will hand it over to him here."

Not a word of her adventure; nor so much as one glance at Mr. Van Broecklyn, standing far back in the shadows.

*****

Nor was she more communicative, when, the

formula restored and everything made right with Mr. Spielhagen, they all came together again in the library for a final word.

"I was frightened by the silence and the darkness, and so cried out," she explained in answer to their questions. "Anyone would have done so who found himself alone in so musty a place," she added, with an attempt at lightsomeness which deepened the pallor on Mr. Van Broecklyn's cheek, already sufficiently noticeable to have been remarked upon by more than one.

"No ghosts?" laughed Mr. Cornell, too happy in the return of his hopes to be fully sensible of the feelings of those about him. "No whispers from impalpable lips or touches from spectre hands? Nothing to explain the mystery of that room so long shut up that even Mr. Van Broecklyn declares himself ignorant of its secret?"

"Nothing," returned Violet, showing her dimples in full force now.

"If Miss Strange had any such experiences — if she has anything to tell worthy of so marked a curiosity, she will tell it now," came from the gentleman just alluded to, in tones so stern and strange that all show of frivolity ceased on the instant. "Have you anything to tell, Miss Strange?"

Greatly startled, she regarded him with widening eyes for a moment, then with a move towards the door, remarked, with a general look about her:

"Mr. Van Broecklyn knows his own house, and doubtless can relate its histories if he will. I am a busy little body who having finished my work am now ready to return home, there to wait for the next problem which an indulgent fate may offer me."

She was near the threshold — she was about to take her leave, when suddenly she felt two hands fall on her shoulder, and turning, met the eyes of Mr. Van Broecklyn burning into her own.

"*You saw!*" dropped in an almost inaudible whisper from his lips.

The shiver which shook her answered him better than any word.

With an exclamation of despair, he withdrew his hands, and facing the others now standing together recovered some of his self-possession:

"I must ask for another hour of your company. I can no longer keep my sorrow to myself. A dividing line has just been drawn across my life, and I must have the sympathy of someone who knows my past, or I shall go mad in my self-imposed solitude. Come back, Miss Strange. You of all others have the prior right to hear."

VII

"I shall have to begin," said he, when they were all seated and ready to listen, "by giving you some idea, not so much of the family tradition, as of the effect of this tradition upon all who bore the name of Van Broecklyn. This is not the only house, even in America, which contains a room shut away from intrusion. In England there are many. But there is this difference between most of them and ours. No bars or locks forcibly held shut the door we were forbidden to open. The command was enough; that and the superstitious fear which such a command, attended by a long and unquestioning obedience, was likely to engender.

"I know no more than you do why some early

ancestor laid his ban upon this room. But from my earliest years I was given to understand that there was one latch in the house which was never to be lifted; that any fault would be forgiven sooner than that; that the honour of the whole family stood in the way of disobedience, and that I was to preserve that honour to my dying day. You will say that all this is fantastic, and wonder that sane people in these modern times should subject themselves to such a ridiculous restriction, especially when no good reason was alleged, and the very source of the tradition from which it sprung forgotten. You are right; but if you look long into human nature, you will see that the bonds which hold the firmest are not material ones — that an idea will make a man and mould a character — that it lies at the source of all heroisms and is to be courted or feared as the case may be.

"For me it possessed a power proportionate to my loneliness. I don't think there was ever a more lonely child. My father and mother were so unhappy in each other's companionship that one or other of them was almost always away. But I saw little of either even when they were at home. The constraint in their attitude toward each other affected their conduct toward me. I have asked myself more than once if either of them had any real affection for me. To my father I spoke of her; to her of him; and never pleasurably. This I am forced to say, or you cannot understand my story. Would to God I could tell another tale! Would to God I had such memories as other men have of a father's clasp, a mother's kiss — but no! my grief, already profound, might have become abysmal. Perhaps it is best as it is; only, I might have been a different child, and made for myself a different fate — who knows.

"As it was, I was thrown almost entirely upon my own resources for any amusement. This led me to a discovery I made one day. In a far part of the cellar behind some heavy casks, I found a little door. It was so low — so exactly fitted to my small body, that I had the greatest desire to enter it. But I could not get around the casks. At last an expedient occurred to me. We had an old servant who came nearer loving me than anyone else. One day when I chanced to be alone in the cellar, I took out my ball and began throwing it about. Finally it landed behind the casks, and I ran with a beseeching cry to Michael, to move them.

"It was a task requiring no little strength and address, but he managed, after a few herculean efforts, to shift them aside and I saw with delight my way opened to that mysterious little door. But I did not approach it then; some instinct deterred me. But when the opportunity came for me to venture there alone, I did so, in the most adventurous spirit, and began my operations by sliding behind the casks and testing the handle of the little door. It turned, and after a pull or two the door yielded. With my heart in my mouth, I stooped and peered in. I could see nothing — a black hole and nothing more. This caused me a moment's hesitation. I was afraid of the dark — had always been. But curiosity and the spirit of adventure triumphed. Saying to myself that I was Robinson Crusoe exploring the cave, I crawled in, only to find that I had gained nothing. It was as dark inside as it had looked to be from without.

"There was no fun in this, so I crawled back and when I tried the experiment again, it was with a bit of candle in my hand, and a surreptitious match or two. What I saw, when with a very trembling little hand I had lighted one of the matches, would have been disappointing to most boys, but not to me. The litter and old boards I saw in odd corners about me were full of possibilities, while in the dimness beyond I seemed to perceive a sort of staircase which might lead — I do not think I made any attempt to answer that question even in my own mind, but when, after some hesitation and a sense of great daring, I finally crept up those steps, I remember very well my sensation at finding myself in front of a narrow closed door. It suggested too vividly the one in Grandfather's little room — the door in the wainscot which we were never to open. I had my first real trembling fit here, and at once fascinated and repelled by this obstruction I stumbled and lost my candle, which, going out in the fall, left me in total darkness and a very frightened state of mind. For my imagination, which had been greatly stirred by my own vague thoughts of the forbidden room, immediately began to people the space about me with ghoulish figures. How should I escape them, how ever reach my own little room again, undetected and in safety?

"But these terrors, deep as they were, were nothing to the real fright which seized me when, the darkness finally braved, and the way found back into the bright, wide-open halls of the house, I became conscious of having dropped something besides the candle. My match-box was gone — not *my* match-box, but my grandfather's which I had found lying on his table and carried off on this adventure, in all the confidence of irresponsible youth. To make use of it for a little while, trusting to his not missing it in the confusion I had noticed about the house that morning, was one thing; to lose it was another. It was no common box. Made of gold and cherished for some special reason well known to himself, I had often heard him say that some day I would appreciate its value and be glad to own it. And I had left it in that hole and at any minute he might miss it — possibly ask for it! The day was one of torment. My mother was away or shut up in her room. My father — I don't know just what thoughts I had about him. He was not to be seen either, and the servants cast strange looks at me when I spoke his name. But I little realized the blow which had just fallen upon the house in his definite departure, and only thought of my own trouble, and of how I should meet my grandfather's eye when the hour came for him to draw me to his knee for his usual goodnight.

"That I was spared this ordeal for the first time this very night first comforted me, then added to my distress. He had discovered his loss and was angry. On the morrow he would ask me for the box and I would have to lie, for never could I find the courage to tell him where I had been. Such an act of presumption he would never forgive, or so I thought as I lay and shivered in my little bed. That his coldness, his neglect, sprang from the discovery just made that my mother as well as my father had just fled the house forever was as little known to me as the morning calamity. I had been given my usual tendance and was tucked safely into bed; but the gloom, the silence which presently settled upon the house had a very different explanation in my mind from the real one. My sin (for such it loomed large in my mind by this time) coloured the whole situation and accounted for every event.

"At what hour I slipped from my bed on to the cold floor, I shall never know. To me it seemed to be in the dead of night; but I doubt if it were more than ten. So slowly creep away the moments to a wakeful child. I had made a great resolve. Awful as the prospect seemed to me, — frightened as I was by the very thought, — I had determined in my small mind to go down into the cellar, and into that midnight hole again, in search of the lost box. I would take a candle and matches, this time from my own mantel-shelf, and if everyone was asleep, as appeared from the deathly quiet of the house, I would be able to go and come without anybody ever being the wiser.

"Dressing in the dark, I found my matches and my candle and, putting them in one of my pockets, softly opened my door and looked out. Nobody was stirring; every light was out except a solitary one in the lower hall. That this still burned conveyed no meaning to my mind. How could I know that the house was so still and the rooms so dark because everyone was out searching for some clue to my mother's flight? If I had looked at the clock — but I did not; I was too intent upon my errand, too filled with the fever of my desperate undertaking, to be affected by anything not bearing directly upon it.

"Of the terror caused by my own shadow on the wall as I made the turn in the hall below, I have as keen a recollection to-day as though it happened yesterday. But that did not deter me; nothing deterred me, till safe in the cellar I crouched down behind the casks to get my breath again before entering the hole beyond.

"I had made some noise in feeling my way around these casks, and I trembled lest these sounds had been heard upstairs! But this fear soon gave place to one far greater. Other sounds were making themselves heard. A din of small skurrying feet above, below, on every side of me! Rats! rats in the wall! rats on the cellar bottom! How I ever stirred from the spot I do not know, but when I did stir, it was to go forward, and enter the uncanny hole.

"I had intended to light my candle when I got inside; but for some reason I went stumbling along in the dark, following the wall till I got to the steps where I had dropped the box. Here a light was necessary, but my hand did not go to my pocket. I thought it better to climb the steps first, and softly one foot found the tread and then another. I had only three more to climb and then my right hand, now feeling its way along the wall, would be free to strike a match. I climbed the three steps and was steadying myself against the door for a final plunge, when something happened — something so strange, so unexpected, and so incredible that I wonder I did not shriek aloud in my terror. The door was moving under my hand. It was slowly opening inward. I could feel the chill made by the widening crack. Moment by moment this chill increased; the gap was growing — a presence was there — a presence before which I sank in a small heap upon the landing. Would it advance? Had it feet — hands? Was it a presence which could be felt?

"Whatever it was, it made no attempt to pass, and presently I lifted my head only to quake anew at the sound of a voice — a human voice — my mother's voice — so near me that by putting out my arms I might have touched her.

"She was speaking to my father. I knew it from the tone. She was saying words which, little understood as they were, made such a havoc in my youthful mind that I have never forgotten them.

"'I have come!' she said. 'They think I have fled

the house and are looking far and wide for me. We shall not be disturbed. Who would think of looking here for either you or me?'

"*Here!* The word sank like a plummet in my breast. I had known for some few minutes that I was on the threshold of the forbidden room; but they were *in* it. I can scarcely make you understand the tumult which this awoke in my brain. Somehow, I had never thought that any such braving of the house's law would be possible.

"I heard my father's answer, but it conveyed no meaning to me. I also realized that he spoke from a distance, — that he was at one end of the room while we were at the other. I was presently to have this idea confirmed, for while I was striving with all my might and main to subdue my very heart-throbs so that she would not hear me or suspect my presence, the darkness — I should rather say the blackness of the place yielded to a flash of lightning — heat lightning, all glare and no sound — and I caught an instantaneous vision of my father's figure standing with gleaming things about him, which affected me at the moment as supernatural, but which, in later years, I decided to have been weapons hanging on a wall.

"She saw him too, for she gave a quick laugh and said they would not need any candles; and then, there was another flash and I saw something in his hand and something in hers, and though I did not yet understand, I felt myself turning deathly sick and gave a choking gasp which was lost in the rush she made into the centre of the room, and the keenness of her swift low cry.

"'*Garde-toi!* for only one of us will ever leave this room alive!'

"A duel! a duel to the death between this husband and wife — this father and mother — in this hole of dead tragedies and within the sight and hearing of their child! Has Satan ever devised a scheme more hideous for ruining the life of an eleven-year-old boy!

"Not that I took it all in at once. I was too innocent and much too dazed to comprehend such hatred, much less the passions which engendered it. I only knew that something horrible — something beyond the conception of my childish mind — was going to take place in the darkness before me; and the terror of it made me speechless; would to God it had made me deaf and blind and dead!

"She had dashed from her corner and he had slid away from his, as the next fantastic gleam which lit up the room showed me. It also showed the weapons in their hands, and for a moment I felt reassured when I saw these were swords, for I had seen them before with foils in their hands practising for exercise, as they said, in the great garret. But the swords had buttons on them, and this time the tips were sharp and shone in the keen light.

"An exclamation from her and a growl of rage from him were followed by movements I could scarcely hear, but which were terrifying from their very quiet. Then the sound of a clash. The swords had crossed.

"Had the lightning flashed forth then, the end of one of them might have occurred. But the darkness remained undisturbed, and when the glare relit the great room again, they were already far apart. This called out a word from him; the one sentence he spoke — I can never forget it:

"'Rhoda, there is blood on your sleeve; I have wounded you. Shall we call it off and fly, as the poor creatures in there think we have, to the opposite ends of the earth?'

"I almost spoke; I almost added my childish plea to his for them to stop — to remember me and stop. But not a muscle in my throat responded to my agonized effort. Her cold, clear 'No!' fell before my tongue was loosed or my heart freed from the ponderous weight crushing it.

"'I have vowed and *I* keep my promises,' she went on in a tone quite strange to me. 'What would either's life be worth with the other alive and happy in this world?'

"He made no answer; and those subtle movements — shadows of movements I might almost call them — recommenced. Then there came a sudden cry, shrill and poignant — had Grandfather been in his room he would surely have heard it — and the flash coming almost simultaneously with its utterance, I saw what has haunted my sleep from that day to this, my father pinned against the wall, sword still in hand, and before him my mother, fiercely triumphant, her staring eyes fixed on his and —

"Nature could bear no more; the band loosened from my throat; the oppression lifted from my breast long enough for me to give one wild wail and she turned, saw (heaven sent its flashes quickly at this moment) and recognizing my childish form, all the horror of her deed (or so I have fondly hoped) rose within her, and she gave a start and fell full upon the point upturned to receive her.

"A groan; then a gasping sigh from him, and silence settled upon the room and upon my heart and so far as I knew upon the whole created world.

*****

"That is my story, friends. Do you wonder that I have never been or lived like other men?"

After a few moments of sympathetic silence, Mr. Van Broecklyn went on to say:

"I don't think I ever had a moment's doubt that my parents both lay dead on the floor of that great room. When I came to myself — which may have been soon, and may not have been for a long while — the lightning had ceased to flash, leaving the darkness stretching like a blank pall between me and that spot in which were concentrated all the terrors of which my imagination was capable. I dared not enter it. I dared not take one step that way. My instinct was to fly and hide my trembling body again in my own bed; and associated with this, in fact dominating it and making me old before my time, was another — never to tell; never to let anyone, least of all my grandfather — know what that forbidden room now contained. I felt in an irresistible sort of way that my father's and mother's honour was at stake. Besides, terror held me back; I felt that I should die if I spoke. Childhood has such terrors and such heroisms. Silence often covers in such, abysses of thought and feeling which astonish us in later years. There is no suffering like a child's, terrified by a secret it dare not for some reason disclose.

"Events aided me. When, in desperation to see once more the light and all the things which linked me to life — my little bed, the toys on the windowsill, my squirrel in its cage — I forced myself to retraverse the empty house, expecting at every turn to hear my father's voice or come upon the image of my mother — yes, such was the confusion of my mind, though I knew well enough even then that they were dead and that I should never hear the one or see the other. I was so benumbed with the cold in my half-dressed condition, that I woke in a fever next morning after a terrible dream which forced from my lips the cry of 'Mother! Mother!' — only that.

"I was cautious even in delirium. This delirium and my flushed cheeks and shining eyes led them to be very careful to me. I was told that my mother was away from home; and when after two days of search they were quite sure that all efforts to find either her or my father were likely to prove fruitless, that she had gone to Europe where we would follow her as soon as I was well. This promise, offering as it did, a prospect of immediate release from the terrors which were consuming me, had an extraordinary effect upon me. I got up out of my bed saying that I was well now and ready to start on the instant. The doctor, finding my pulse equable, and my whole condition wonderfully improved, and attributing it, as was natural, to my hope of soon joining my mother, advised my whim to be humoured and this hope kept active till travel and intercourse with children should give me strength and prepare me for the bitter truth ultimately awaiting me. They listened to him and in twenty-four hours our preparations were made. We saw the house closed — with what emotions surging in one small breast, I leave you to imagine — and then started on our long tour. For five years we wandered over the continent of Europe, my grandfather finding distraction, as well as myself, in foreign scenes and associations.

"But return was inevitable. What I suffered on re-entering this house, God and my sleepless pillow alone know. Had any discovery been made in our absence; or would it be made now that renovation and repairs of all kinds were necessary? Time finally answered me. My secret was safe and likely to continue so, and this fact once settled, life became endurable, if not cheerful. Since then I have spent only two nights out of this house, and they were unavoidable. When my grandfather died I had the wainscot door cemented in. It was done from this side and the cement painted to match the wood. No one opened the door nor have I ever crossed its threshold. Sometimes I think I have been foolish; and sometimes I know that I have been very wise. My reason has stood firm; how do I know that it would have done so if I had subjected myself to the possible discovery that one or both of them might have been saved if I had disclosed instead of concealed my adventure."

*****

A pause during which white horror had shone on every face; then with a final glance at Violet, he said:

"What sequel do you see to this story, Miss Strange? I can tell the past, I leave you to picture the future."

Rising, she let her eye travel from face to face till it rested on the one awaiting it, when she answered dreamily:

"If some morning in the news column there should appear an account of the ancient and historic home of the Van Broecklyns having burned to the ground in the night, the whole country would mourn, and the city feel defrauded of one of its treasures. But there are five persons who would see in it the sequel which you ask for."

When this happened, as it did happen, some few weeks later, the astonishing discovery was made that no insurance had been put upon this house. Why was it that after such a loss Mr. Van Broecklyn seemed to renew his youth? It was a constant source of comment among his friends.

V. A Scandal in Bohemia — A. Conan Doyle

I

To Sherlock Holmes she is always *the* woman. I have seldom heard him mention her under any other name. In his eyes she eclipses and predominates the whole of her sex. It was not that he felt any emotion akin to love for Irene Adler. All emotions, and that one particularly, were abhorrent to his cold, precise but admirably balanced mind. He was, I take it, the most perfect reasoning and observing machine that the world has seen; but as a lover, he would have placed himself in a false position. He never spoke of the softer passions, save with a gibe and a sneer. They were admirable things for the observer — excellent for drawing the veil from men's motives and actions. But for the trained reasoner to admit such intrusions into his own delicate and finely adjusted temperament was to introduce a distracting factor which might throw a doubt upon all his mental results. Grit in a sensitive instrument, or a crack in one of his own high-power lenses, would not be more disturbing than a strong emotion in a nature such as his. And yet there was but one woman to him, and that woman was the late Irene Adler, of dubious and questionable memory.

I had seen little of Holmes lately. My marriage had drifted us away from each other. My own complete happiness, and the home-centred interests which rise up around the man who first finds himself master of his own establishment, were sufficient to absorb all my attention; while Holmes, who loathed every form of society with his whole Bohemian soul, remained in our lodgings in Baker Street, buried among his old books, and alternating from week to week between cocaine and ambition, the drowsiness of the drug and the fierce energy of his own keen nature. He was still, as ever, deeply attracted by the study of crime, and occupied his immense faculties and extraordinary powers of observation in following out those clews, and clearing up those mysteries, which had been abandoned as hopeless by the official police. From time to time I heard some vague account of his doings; of his summons to Odessa in the case of the Trepoff murder, of his clearing up of the singular tragedy of the Atkinson brothers at Trincomalee, and finally of the mission which he had accomplished so delicately and successfully for the reigning family of Holland. Beyond these signs of his activity, however, which I merely shared with all the readers of the daily press, I knew little of my former friend and companion.

One night — it was on the 20th of March, 1888 — I was returning from a journey to a patient (for I had now returned to civil practice), when my way led me through Baker Street. As I passed the well-remembered door, which must always be associated in my mind with my wooing, and with the dark incidents of the Study in Scarlet, I was seized with a keen desire to see Holmes again, and to know how he was employing his extraordinary powers. His rooms were brilliantly lighted, and even as I looked up, I saw his tall, spare figure pass twice in a dark silhouette against the blind. He was pacing the room swiftly, eagerly, with his head sunk upon his chest, and his hands clasped behind him. To me, who knew his every mood and habit, his attitude and manner told their own story. He was at work again. He had risen out of his drug-created dreams, and was hot upon the scent of some new problem. I rang the bell, and was shown up to the chamber which had formerly been in part my own.

His manner was not effusive. It seldom was; but he was glad, I think, to see me. With hardly a word spoken, but with a kindly eye, he waved me to an armchair, threw across his case of cigars, and indicated a spirit case and a gasogene in the corner. Then he stood before the fire, and looked me over in his singular introspective fashion.

"Wedlock suits you," he remarked. "I think Watson, that you have put on seven and a half pounds since I saw you."

"Seven," I answered.

"Indeed, I should have thought a little more. Just a trifle more, I fancy, Watson. And in practice again, I observe. You did not tell me that you intended to go into harness."

"Then how do you know?"

"I see it, I deduce it. How do I know that you have been getting yourself very wet lately, and that you have a most clumsy and careless servant girl?"

"My dear Holmes," said I, "this is too much. You would certainly have been burned had you lived a few centuries ago. It is true that I had a country walk on Thursday and came home in a dreadful mess; but as I have changed my clothes, I can't imagine how you deduce it. As to Mary Jane, she is incorrigible, and my wife has given her notice; but there again I fail to see how you work it out."

He chuckled to himself and rubbed his long nervous hands together.

"It is simplicity itself," said he, "my eyes tell me that on the inside of your left shoe, just where the firelight strikes it, the leather is scored by six almost parallel cuts. Obviously they have been caused by someone who has very carelessly scraped round the edges of the sole in order to remove crusted mud from it. Hence, you see, my double deduction that you had been out in vile weather, and that you had a particularly malignant boot-slicking specimen of the London slavey. As to your practice, if a gentleman walks into my rooms, smelling of iodoform, with a black mark of nitrate of silver upon his right forefinger, and a bulge on the side of his top hat to show where he has secreted his stethoscope, I must be dull indeed if I do not pronounce him to be an active member of the medical profession."

I could not help laughing at the ease with which he explained his process of deduction. "When I hear you give your reasons," I remarked, "the thing always appears to me so ridiculously simple that I could easily do it myself, though at each successive instance of your reasoning I am baffled, until you explain your process. And yet, I believe that my eyes are as good as yours."

"Quite so," he answered, lighting a cigarette, and throwing himself down into an armchair. "You see, but you do not observe. The distinction is clear. For example, you have frequently seen the steps which lead up from the hall to this room."

"Frequently."

"How often?"

"Well, some hundreds of times."

"Then how many are there?"

"How many? I don't know."

"Quite so! You have not observed. And yet you have seen. That is just my point. Now, I know there are seventeen steps, because I have both seen and observed. By the way, since you are interested in these little problems, and since you are good enough to chronicle one or two of my trifling experiences, you may be interested in this." He threw over a sheet of thick pink-tinted note paper which had been lying open upon the table. "It came by the last post," said he. "Read it aloud."

The note was undated, and without either signature or address.

"There will call upon you to-night, at a quarter to eight o'clock," it said, "a gentleman who desires to consult you upon a matter of the very deepest moment. Your recent services to one of the royal houses of Europe have shown that you are one who may safely be trusted with matters which are of an importance which can hardly be exaggerated. This account of you we have from all quarters received. Be in your chamber, then, at that hour, and do not take it amiss if your visitor wears a mask."

"This is indeed a mystery," I remarked. "What do you imagine that it means?"

"I have no data yet. It is a capital mistake to theorize before one has data. Insensibly one begins to twist facts to suit theories, instead of theories to suit facts. But the note itself — what do you deduce from it?"

I carefully examined the writing, and the paper upon which it was written.

"The man who wrote it was presumably well to do," I remarked, endeavouring to imitate my companion's processes. "Such paper could not be bought under half a crown a packet. It is peculiarly strong and stiff."

"Peculiar — that is the very word," said Holmes. "It is not an English paper at all. Hold it up to the light."

I did so, and saw a large *E* with a small *g*, a *P* and a large *G* with a small *t* woven into the texture of the paper.

"What do you make of that?" asked Holmes.

"The name of the maker, no doubt; or his monogram, rather."

"Not all. The *G* with the small *t* stands for 'Gesellschaft,' which is the German for 'Company.' It is a customary contraction like our 'Co.' *P*, of course, stands for 'Papier.' Now for the *Eg*. Let us glance at our 'Continental Gazetteer.'" He took down a heavy brown volume from his shelves. "Eglow, Eglonitz — here we are, Egria. It is in a German-speaking country — in Bohemia, not far from Carlsbad. 'Remarkable as being the scene of the death of Wallenstein, and for its numerous glass factories and paper mills.' Ha! ha! my boy, what do you make of that?" His eyes sparkled, and he sent up a great blue triumphant cloud from his cigarette.

"The paper was made in Bohemia," I said.

"Precisely. And the man who wrote the note is a German. Do you note the peculiar construction of the sentence — 'This account of you we have from all quarters received'? A Frenchman or Russian could not have written that. It is the German who is so uncourteous to his verbs. It only remains, therefore, to discover what is wanted by this German who writes upon Bohemian paper, and prefers wearing a mask to showing his face. And here he comes, if I am not mistaken, to resolve all our doubts."

As he spoke there was the sharp sound of horses' hoofs and grating wheels against the curb, followed by a sharp pull at the bell. Holmes whistled.

"A pair, by the sound," said he. "Yes," he continued, glancing out of the window. "A nice little brougham and a pair of beauties. A hundred and fifty guineas apiece. There's money in this case, Watson, if there is nothing else."

"I think I had better go, Holmes."

"Not a bit, doctor. Stay where you are. I am lost without my Boswell. And this promises to be interesting. It would be a pity to miss it."

"But your client — "

"Never mind him. I may want your help, and so may he. Here he comes. Sit down in that armchair, doctor, and give us your best attention."

A slow and heavy step, which had been heard upon the stairs and in the passage, paused immediately outside the door. Then there was a loud and authoritative tap.

"Come in!" said Holmes.

A man entered who could hardly have been less than six feet six inches in height, with the chest and limbs of a Hercules. His dress was rich with a richness which would, in England, be looked upon as akin to bad taste. Heavy bands of astrakhan were slashed across the sleeves and front of his double-breasted coat, while the deep blue cloak which was thrown over his shoulders was lined with flame-coloured silk, and secured at the neck with a brooch which consisted of a single flaming beryl. Boots which extended halfway up his calves, and which were trimmed at the tops with rich brown fur, completed the impression of barbaric opulence which was suggested by his whole appearance. He carried a broad-brimmed hat in his hand, while he wore across the upper part of his face, extending down past the cheek-bones, a black visard mask, which he had apparently adjusted that very moment, for his hand was still raised to it as he entered. From the lower part of the face he appeared to be a man of strong character, with a thick, hanging lip, and a long, straight chin, suggestive of resolution pushed to the length of obstinacy.

"You had my note?" he asked, with a deep, harsh voice and a strongly marked German accent. "I told you that I would call." He looked from one to the other of us, as if uncertain which to address.

"Pray take a seat," said Holmes. "This is my friend and colleague, Doctor Watson, who is occasionally good enough to help me in my cases. Whom have I the honour to address?"

"You may address me as the Count von Kramm, a Bohemian nobleman. I understand that this gentleman, your friend, is a man of honour and discretion, whom I may trust with a matter of the most extreme importance. If not I should much prefer to communicate with you alone."

I rose to go, but Holmes caught me by the wrist and pushed me back into my chair. "It is both, or none," said he. "You may say before this gentleman anything which you may say to me."

The count shrugged his broad shoulders. "Then I must begin," said he, "by binding you both to absolute secrecy for two years; at the end of that time the matter will be of no importance. At present it is not too much to say that it is of such weight that it may have an influence upon European history."

"I promise," said Holmes.

"And I."

"You will excuse this mask," continued our strange visitor. "The august person who employs me wishes his agent to be unknown to you, and I may confess at once that the title by which I have just called myself is not exactly my own."

"I was aware of it," said Holmes, dryly.

"The circumstances are of great delicacy, and every precaution has to be taken to quench what might grow to be an immense scandal, and seriously compromise one of the reigning families of Europe. To speak plainly, the matter implicates the great House of Ormstein, hereditary kings of Bohemia."

"I was also aware of that," murmured Holmes, settling himself down in his armchair, and closing his eyes.

Our visitor glanced with some apparent surprise at the languid, lounging figure of the man who had been, no doubt, depicted to him as the most incisive reasoner and most energetic agent in Europe. Holmes slowly reopened his eyes and looked impatiently at his gigantic client.

"If your majesty would condescend to state your case," he remarked, "I should be better able to advise you."

The man sprung from his chair, and paced up and down the room in uncontrollable agitation. Then, with a gesture of desperation, he tore the mask from his face and hurled it upon the ground.

"You are right," he cried, "I am the king. Why should I attempt to conceal it?"

"Why, indeed?" murmured Holmes. "Your majesty had not spoken before I was aware that I was addressing Wilhelm Gottsreich Sigismond von Ormstein, Grand Duke of Cassel-Felstein, and hereditary King of Bohemia."

"But you can understand," said our strange visitor, sitting down once more and passing his hand over his high, white forehead, "you can understand that I am not accustomed to doing such business in my own person. Yet the matter was so delicate that I could not confide it to an agent without putting myself in his power. I have come incognito from Prague for the purpose of consulting you."

"Then, pray consult," said Holmes, shutting his eyes once more.

"The facts are briefly these: Some five years ago, during a lengthy visit to Warsaw, I made the acquaintance of the well-known adventuress Irene Adler. The name is no doubt familiar to you."

"Kindly look her up in my index, doctor," murmured Holmes, without opening his eyes. For many years he had adopted a system for docketing all paragraphs concerning men and things, so that it was difficult to name a subject or a person on which he could not at once furnish information. In this case I found her biography sandwiched in between that of a Hebrew rabbi and that of a staff commander who had written a monograph upon the deep-sea fishes.

"Let me see!" said Holmes. "Hum! Born in New

Jersey in the year 1858. Contralto — hum! La Scala — hum! Prima donna Imperial Opera of Warsaw — yes! Retired from operatic stage — ha! Living in London — quite so! Your majesty, as I understand, became entangled with this young person, wrote her some compromising letters, and is now desirous of getting those letters back."

"Precisely so. But how — "

"Was there a secret marriage?"

"None."

"No legal papers or certificates?"

"None."

"Then I fail to follow your majesty. If this young person should produce her letters for blackmailing or other purposes, how is she to prove their authenticity?"

"There is the writing."

"Pooh-pooh! Forgery."

"My private note paper."

"Stolen."

"My own seal."

"Imitated."

"My photograph."

"Bought."

"We were both in the photograph."

"Oh, dear! That is very bad. Your majesty has indeed committed an indiscretion."

"I was mad — insane."

"You have compromised yourself seriously."

"I was only crown prince then. I was young. I am but thirty now."

"It must be recovered."

"We have tried and failed."

"Your majesty must pay. It must be bought."

"She will not sell."

"Stolen, then."

"Five attempts have been made. Twice burglars in my pay ransacked her house. Once we diverted her luggage when she travelled. Twice she has been waylaid. There has been no result."

"No sign of it?"

"Absolutely none."

Holmes laughed. "It is quite a pretty little problem," said he.

"But a very serious one to me," returned the king, reproachfully.

"Very, indeed. And what does she propose to do with the photograph?"

"To ruin me."

"But how?"

"I am about to be married."

"So I have heard."

"To Clotilde Lothman von Saxe-Meiningen, second daughter of the King of Scandinavia. You may know the strict principles of her family. She is herself the very soul of delicacy. A shadow of a doubt as to my conduct would bring the matter to an end."

"And Irene Adler?"

"Threatens to send them the photograph. And she will do it. I know that she will do it. You do not know her, but she has a soul of steel. She has the face of the most beautiful of women and the mind of the most resolute of men. Rather than I should marry another woman, there are no lengths to which she would not go — none."

"You are sure she has not sent it yet?"

"I am sure."

"And why?"

"Because she has said that she would send it on the day when the betrothal was publicly proclaimed. That will be next Monday."

"Oh, then we have three days yet," said Holmes, with a yawn. "That is very fortunate, as I have one or two matters of importance to look into just at present. Your majesty will, of course, stay in London for the present?"

"Certainly. You will find me at the Langham, under the name of the Count von Kramm."

"Then I shall drop you a line to let you know how we progress."

"Pray do so; I shall be all anxiety."

"Then, as to money?"

"You have *carte blanche*."

"Absolutely?"

"I tell you that I would give one of the provinces of my kingdom to have that photograph."

"And for present expenses?"

The king took a heavy chamois-leather bag from under his cloak, and laid it on the table.

"There are three hundred pounds in gold, and seven hundred in notes," he said.

Holmes scribbled a receipt upon a sheet of his notebook, and handed it to him.

"And mademoiselle's address?" he asked.

"Is Briony Lodge, Serpentine Avenue, St. John's Wood."

Holmes took a note of it. "One other question," said he, thoughtfully. "Was the photograph a cabinet?"

"It was."

"Then, good-night, your majesty, and I trust that we shall soon have some good news for you. And good-night, Watson," he added, as the wheels of the royal brougham rolled down the street. "If you will be good enough to call to-morrow afternoon, at three o'clock, I should like to chat this little matter over with you."

II

At three o'clock precisely I was at Baker Street, but Holmes had not yet returned. The landlady informed me that he had left the house shortly after eight o'clock in the morning. I sat down beside the fire, however, with the intention of awaiting him, however long he might be. I was already deeply interested in his inquiry, for, though it was surrounded by none of the grim and strange features which were associated with the two crimes which I have already recorded, still, the nature of the case and the exalted station of his client gave it a character of its own. Indeed, apart from the nature of the investigation which my friend had on hand, there was something in his masterly grasp of a situation, and his keen, incisive reasoning, which made it a pleasure to me to study his system of work, and to follow the quick subtle methods by which he disentangled the most inextricable mysteries. So accustomed was I to his invariable success that the very possibility of his failing had ceased to enter into my head.

It was close upon four before the door opened, and a drunken-looking groom, ill-kempt and side-whiskered, with an inflamed face and disreputable clothes, walked into the room. Accustomed as I was to my friend's amazing powers in the use of disguises, I had to look three times before I was certain that it was indeed he. With a nod he vanished into the bedroom, whence he emerged in five minutes tweed-suited and respectable, as of old. Putting his hands into his pockets, he stretched out his legs in front of the fire, and laughed heartily for some minutes.

"Well, really!" he cried, and then he choked, and laughed again until he was obliged to lie back, limp and helpless, in the chair.

"What is it?"

"It's quite too funny. I am sure you could never guess how I employed my morning, or what I ended by doing."

"I can't imagine. I suppose that you have been watching the habits, and, perhaps, the house, of Miss Irene Adler."

"Quite so, but the sequel was rather unusual. I will tell you, however. I left the house a little after eight o'clock this morning in the character of a groom out of work. There is a wonderful sympathy and freemasonry among horsey men. Be one of them, and you will know all that there is to know. I soon found Briony Lodge. It is a bijou villa, with a garden at the back, but built out in the front right up to the road, two stories. Chubb lock to the door. Large sitting room on the right side, well furnished, with long windows almost to the floor, and those preposterous English window fasteners which a child could open. Behind there was nothing remarkable, save that the passage window could be reached from the top of the coach-house. I walked round it and examined it closely from every point of view, but without noting anything else of interest.

"I then lounged down the street, and found, as I expected, that there was a mews in a lane which runs down by one wall of the garden. I lent the hostlers a hand in rubbing down their horses, and I received in exchange two-pence, a glass of half and half, two fills of shag tobacco, and as much information as I could desire about Miss Adler, to say nothing of half a dozen other people in the neighbourhood, in whom I was not in the least interested, but whose biographies I was compelled to listen to."

"And what of Irene Adler?" I asked.

"Oh, she has turned all the men's heads down in that part. She is the daintest thing under a bonnet on this planet. So say the Serpentine Mews, to a man. She lives quietly, sings at concerts, drives out at five every day, and returns at seven sharp for dinner. Seldom goes out at other times, except when she sings. Has only one male visitor, but a good deal of him. He is dark, handsome, and dashing; never calls less than once a day, and often twice. He is a Mr. Godfrey Norton of the Inner Temple. See the advantages of a cabman as a confidant. They had driven him home a dozen times from Serpentine Mews, and knew all about him. When I had listened to all that they had to tell, I began to walk up and down near Briony Lodge once more, and to think over my plan of campaign.

"This Godfrey Norton was evidently an important factor in the matter. He was a lawyer. That sounded ominous. What was the relation between them, and what the object of his repeated visits? Was she his client, his friend, or his mistress? If the former, she had probably transferred the photograph to his keeping. If the latter, it was less likely. On the issue of this question depended whether I should continue my work at Briony Lodge, or turn my attention to the gentleman's chambers in the Temple. It was a delicate point, and it widened the field of my inquiry. I fear that I bore you with these details, but I have to let you see my little difficulties, if you are to understand the situation."

"I am following you closely," I answered.

"I was still balancing the matter in my mind, when a hansom cab drove up to Briony Lodge, and a gentleman sprung out. He was a remarkably handsome man, dark, aquiline, and moustached — evidently the man of whom I had heard. He appeared to be in a great hurry, shouted to the cabman to wait, and brushed past the maid who opened the door, with the air of a man who was thoroughly at home.

"He was in the house about half an hour, and I could catch glimpses of him in the windows of the sitting room, pacing up and down, talking excitedly and waving his arms. Of her I could see nothing. Presently he emerged, looking even more flurried than before. As he stepped up to the cab, he pulled a gold watch from his pocket and looked at it earnestly. 'Drive like the devil!' he shouted, 'first to Gross & Hankey's in Regent Street, and then to the Church of St. Monica in the Edgeware Road. Half a guinea if you do it in twenty minutes!'

"Away they went, and I was just wondering whether I should not do well to follow them, when up the lane came a neat little landau, the coachman with his coat only half buttoned, and his tie under his ear, while all the tags of his harness were sticking out of the buckles. It hadn't pulled up before she shot out of the hall door and into it. I only caught a glimpse of her at the moment, but she was a lovely woman, with a face that a man might die for.

"'The Church of St. Monica, John,' she cried; 'and half a sovereign if you reach it in twenty minutes.'

"This was quite too good to lose, Watson. I was just balancing whether I should run for it, or whether I should perch behind her landau, when a cab came through the street. The driver looked twice at such a shabby fare; but I jumped in before he could object. 'The Church of St. Monica,' said I, 'and half a sovereign if you reach it in twenty minutes.' It was twenty-five minutes to twelve, and of course it was clear enough what was in the wind.

"My cabby drove fast. I don't think I ever drove faster, but the others were there before us. The cab and landau with their steaming horses were in front of the door when I arrived. I paid the man, and hurried into the church. There was not a soul there save the two whom I had followed, and a surpliced clergyman, who seemed to be expostulating with them. They were all three standing in a knot in front of the altar. I lounged up the side aisle like any other idler who has dropped into a church. Suddenly, to my surprise, the three at the altar faced round to me, and Godfrey Norton came running as hard as he could toward me.

"'Thank God!' he cried. 'You'll do. Come! Come!'

"'What then?' I asked.

"'Come, man, come; only three minutes, or it won't be legal.'

"I was half dragged up to the altar, and, before I knew where I was, I found myself mumbling responses which were whispered in my ear, and vouching for things of which I knew nothing, and generally assisting in the secure tying up of Irene Adler, spinster, to Godfrey Norton, bachelor. It was all done in an instant, and there was the gentleman thanking me on the one side and the lady on the other, while the clergyman beamed on me in front. It was the most preposterous position in which I ever found myself in my life, and it was the thought of it that started me laughing just now. It seems that there had been some informality about their license; that the clergyman absolutely refused to marry them without a witness of some sort, and that my lucky appearance saved the bridegroom from having to sally out into the streets in search of a best man. The bride gave me a sovereign, and I mean to wear it on my watch chain in memory of the occasion."

"This is a very unexpected turn of affairs," said

I; "and what then?"

"Well, I found my plans very seriously menaced. It looked as if the pair might take an immediate departure, and so necessitate very prompt and energetic measures on my part. At the church door, however, they separated, he driving back to the Temple, and she to her own house. 'I shall drive out in the park at five as usual,' she said, as she left him. I heard no more. They drove away in different directions, and I went off to make my own arrangements."

"Which are?"

"Some cold beef and a glass of beer," he answered, ringing the bell. "I have been too busy to think of food, and I am likely to be busier still this evening. By the way, doctor, I shall want your co-operation."

"I shall be delighted."

"You don't mind breaking the law?"

"Not in the least."

"Nor running a chance of arrest?"

"Not in a good cause."

"Oh, the cause is excellent!"

"Then I am your man."

"I was sure that I might rely on you."

"But what is it you wish?"

"When Mrs. Turner has brought in the tray I will make it clear to you. Now," he said, as he turned hungrily on the simple fare that our landlady had provided, "I must discuss it while I eat, for

I have not much time. It is nearly five now. In two hours we must be on the scene of action. Miss Irene, or Madame, rather, returns from her drive at seven. We must be at Briony Lodge to meet her."

"And what then?"

"You must leave that to me. I have already arranged what is to occur. There is only one point on which I must insist. You must not interfere, come what may. You understand?"

"I am to be neutral?"

"To do nothing whatever. There will probably be some small unpleasantness. Do not join in it. It will end in my being conveyed into the house. Four or five minutes afterwards the sitting-room window will open. You are to station yourself close to that open window."

"Yes."

"You are to watch me, for I will be visible to you."

"Yes."

"And when I raise my hand — so — you will throw into the room what I give you to throw, and will, at the same time, raise the cry of fire. You quite follow me?"

"Entirely."

"It is nothing very formidable," he said, taking a long, cigar-shaped roll from his pocket. "It is an ordinary plumber's smoke-rocket, fitted with a cap at either end, to make it self-lighting. Your task is confined to that. When you raise your cry of fire, it will be taken up by quite a number of people. You may then walk to the end of the street, and I will rejoin you in ten minutes. I hope that I have made myself clear?"

"I am to remain neutral, to get near the window, to watch you, and, at the signal, to throw in this object, then to raise the cry of fire and to wait you at the corner of the street."

"Precisely."

"Then you may entirely rely on me."

"That is excellent. I think, perhaps, it is almost time that I prepared for the new rôle I have to play."

He disappeared into his bedroom, and returned in a few minutes in the character of an amiable and simple-minded Nonconformist clergyman. His broad black hat, his baggy trousers, his white tie, his sympathetic smile, and general look of peering and benevolent curiosity were such as Mr. John Hare alone could have equalled. It was not merely that Holmes changed his costume. His expression, his manner, his very soul seemed to vary with every fresh part that he assumed. The stage lost a fine actor, even as science lost an acute reasoner, when he became a specialist in crime.

It was a quarter past six when we left Baker Street, and it still wanted ten minutes to the hour when we found ourselves in Serpentine Avenue. It was already dusk, and the lamps were just being lighted as we paced up and down in front of Briony Lodge, waiting for the coming of its occupant. The house was just such as I had pictured it from Sherlock Holmes's succinct description, but the locality appeared to be less private than I expected. On the contrary, for a small street in a quiet neighbourhood, it was remarkably animated. There was a group of shabbily dressed men smoking and laughing in a corner, a scissors-grinder with his wheel, two guardsmen who were flirting with a nurse-girl, and several well-dressed young men who were lounging up and down with cigars in their mouths.

"You see," remarked Holmes, as we paced to and fro in front of the house, "this marriage rather simplifies matters. The photograph becomes a double-edged weapon now. The chances are that she would be as averse to its being seen by Mr. Godfrey Norton as our client is to its coming to the eyes of his princess. Now the question is — where are we to find the photograph?"

"Where, indeed?"

"It is most unlikely that she carries it about with her. It is cabinet size. Too large for easy concealment about a woman's dress. She knows that the king is capable of having her waylaid and searched. Two attempts of the sort have already been made. We may take it, then, that she does not carry it about with her."

"Where, then?"

"Her banker or her lawyer. There is that double possibility. But I am inclined to think neither. Women are naturally secretive, and they like to do their own secreting. Why should she hand it over to anyone else? She could trust her own guardianship, but she could not tell what indirect or political influence might be brought to bear upon a business man. Besides, remember that she had resolved to use it within a few days. It must be where she can lay her hands upon it. It must be in her own house."

"But it has twice been burglarized."

"Pshaw! They did not know how to look."

"But how will you look?"

"I will not look."

"What then?"

"I will get her to show me."

"But she will refuse."

"She will not be able to. But I hear the rumble of wheels. It is her carriage. Now carry out my orders to the letter."

As he spoke, the gleam of the sidelights of a carriage came round the curve of the avenue. It was a smart little landau which rattled up to the door of Briony Lodge. As it pulled up one of the loafing men at the corner dashed forward to open the door in the hope of earning a copper, but was elbowed away by another loafer who had rushed up with the same intention. A fierce quarrel broke out which was increased by the two guardsmen, who took sides with one of the loungers, and by the scissors grinder, who was equally hot upon the other side. A blow was struck, and in an instant the lady, who had stepped from her carriage, was the centre of a little knot of struggling men who struck savagely at each other with their fists and sticks. Holmes dashed into the crowd to protect the lady; but, just as he reached her, he gave a cry and dropped to the ground, with the blood running freely down his face. At his fall the guardsmen took to their heels in one direction and the loungers in the other, while a number of better-dressed people who had watched the scuffle without taking part in it crowded in to help the lady and to attend to the injured man. Irene Adler, as I will still call her, had hurried up the steps; but she stood at the top, with her superb figure outlined against the lights of the hall, looking back into the street.

"Is the poor gentleman much hurt?" she asked.

"He is dead," cried several voices.

"No, no, there's life in him," shouted another. "But he'll be gone before you can get him to the hospital."

"He's a brave fellow," said the woman. "They would have had the lady's purse and watch if it hadn't been for him. They were a gang, and a rough one, too. Ah! he's breathing now."

"He can't lie in the street. May we bring him in, marm?"

"Surely. Bring him into the sitting-room. There is a comfortable sofa. This way, please." Slowly and solemnly he was borne into Briony Lodge, and laid out in the principal room, while I still observed the proceedings from my post by the window. The lamps had been lighted, but the blinds had not been drawn, so that I could see Holmes as he lay upon the couch. I do not know whether he was seized with compunction at that moment for the part he was playing, but I know that I never felt more heartily ashamed of myself in my life than when I saw the beautiful creature against whom I was conspiring, or the grace and kindliness with which she waited upon the injured man. And yet it would be the blackest treachery to Holmes to draw back now from the part which he had intrusted to me. I hardened my heart, and took the smoke-rocket from under my ulster. After all, I thought, we are not injuring her. We are but preventing her from injuring another.

Holmes had sat upon the couch, and I saw him

motion like a man who is in need of air. A maid rushed across and threw open the window. At the same instant I saw him raise his hand, and at the signal I tossed my rocket into the room with a cry of "Fire!" The word was no sooner out of my mouth than the whole crowd of spectators, well dressed and ill — gentlemen, hostlers, and servant maids — joined in a general shriek of "Fire!" Thick clouds of smoke curled through the room, and out at the open window. I caught a glimpse of rushing figures, and a moment later the voice of Holmes from within assuring them that it was a false alarm. Slipping through the shouting crowd, I made my way to the corner of the street, and in ten minutes was rejoiced to find my friend's arm in mine, and to get away from the scene of uproar. He walked swiftly and in silence for some few minutes, until we had turned down one of the quiet streets which led toward the Edgeware Road.

"You did it very nicely, doctor," he remarked. "Nothing could have been better. It is all right."

"You have the photograph?"

"I know where it is."

"And how did you find out?"

"She showed me, as I told you that she would."

"I am still in the dark."

"I do not wish to make a mystery," said he, laughing. "The matter was perfectly simple. You, of course, saw that everyone in the street was an accomplice. They were all engaged for the evening."

"I guessed as much."

"Then, when the row broke out, I had a little

moist red paint in the palm of my hand. I rushed forward, fell down, clapped my hand to my face, and became a piteous spectacle. It is an old trick."

"That also I could fathom."

"Then they carried me in. She was bound to have me in. What else could she do? And into her sitting room, which was the very room which I suspected. It lay between that and her bedroom, and I was determined to see which. They laid me on a couch, I motioned for air, they were compelled to open the window, and you had your chance."

"How did that help you?"

"It was all-important. When a woman thinks that her house is on fire, her instinct is at once to rush to the thing which she values most. It is a perfectly overpowering impulse, and I have more than once taken advantage of it. In the case of the Darlington Substitution Scandal it was of use to me, and also in the Arnsworth Castle business. A married woman grabs at her baby — an unmarried one reaches for her jewel box. Now it was clear to me that our lady of to-day had nothing in the house more precious to her than what we are in quest of. She would rush to secure it. The alarm of fire was admirably done. The smoke and shouting were enough to shake nerves of steel. She responded beautifully. The photograph is in a recess behind a sliding panel just above the right bell-pull. She was there in an instant, and I caught a glimpse of it as she drew it out. When I cried out that it was a false alarm, she replaced it, glanced at the rocket, rushed from the room, and I have not seen her since. I rose, and, making my excuses, escaped from the house. I hesitated whether to attempt to secure the photograph at once; but the coachman had come in, and as he was watching me narrowly, it seemed safer to wait. A little over-precipitance may ruin all."

"And now?" I asked.

"Our quest is practically finished. I shall call with the king to-morrow, and with you, if you care to come with us. We will be shown into the sitting room to wait for the lady, but it is probable that when she comes she may find neither us nor the photograph. It might be a satisfaction to his majesty to regain it with his own hands."

"And when will you call?"

"At eight in the morning. She will not be up, so that we shall have a clear field. Besides, we must be prompt, for this marriage may mean a complete change in her life and habits. I must wire to the king without delay."

We had reached Baker Street, and had stopped at the door. He was searching his pockets for the key when someone passing said:

"Good night, Mister Sherlock Holmes."

There were several people on the pavement at the time, but the greeting appeared to come from a slim youth in an ulster who had hurried by.

"I've heard that voice before," said Holmes staring down the dimly lighted street. "Now, I wonder who the deuce that could have been?"

III

I slept at Baker Street that night, and we were engaged upon our toast and coffee in the morning, when the King of Bohemia rushed into the room.

"You have really got it?" he cried, grasping

Sherlock Holmes by either shoulder, and looking eagerly into his face.

"Not yet."

"But you have hopes?"

"I have hopes."

"Then come. I am all impatience to be gone."

"We must have a cab."

"No, my brougham is waiting."

"Then that will simplify matters." We descended, and started off once more for Briony Lodge.

"Irene Adler is married," remarked Holmes.

"Married! When?"

"Yesterday."

"But to whom?"

"To an English lawyer named Norton."

"But she could not love him."

"I am in hopes that she does."

"And why in hopes?"

"Because it would spare your majesty all fear of future annoyance. If the lady loves her husband, she does not love your majesty. If she does not love your majesty, there is no reason why she should interfere with your majesty's plan."

"It is true. And yet — Well, I wish she had been of my own station. What a queen she would have made!" He relapsed into a moody silence, which was not broken until we drew up in Serpentine Avenue.

The door of Briony Lodge was open, and an elderly woman stood upon the steps. She watched us with a sardonic eye as we stepped from the brougham.

"Mr. Sherlock Holmes, I believe?" said she.

"I am Mr. Holmes," answered my companion, looking at her with a questioning and rather startled gaze.

"Indeed! My mistress told me that you were likely to call. She left this morning with her husband by the 5:15 train from Charing Cross for the Continent."

"What!" Sherlock Holmes staggered back, white with chagrin and surprise. "Do you mean that she has left England?"

"Never to return."

"And the papers?" asked the King, hoarsely. "All is lost."

"We shall see." He pushed past the servant and rushed into the drawing-room, followed by the King and myself. The furniture was scattered about in every direction, with dismantled shelves and open drawers, as if the lady had hurriedly ransacked them before her flight. Holmes rushed at the bell-pull, tore back a small sliding shutter, and, plunging in his hand, pulled out a photograph and a letter. The photograph was of Irene Adler herself in evening dress, the letter was superscribed to "Sherlock Holmes, Esq. To be left till called for." My friend tore it open, and we all three read it together. It was dated at midnight of the preceding night, and ran in this way:

"My dear Mr. Sherlock Holmes, — You really

did it very well. You took me in completely. Until after the alarm of fire, I had not a suspicion. But then, when I found how I had betrayed myself, I began to think. I had been warned against you months ago. I had been told that, if the King employed an agent, it would certainly be you. And your address had been given me. Yet, with all this, you made me reveal what you wanted to know. Even after I became suspicious, I found it hard to think evil of such a dear, kind old clergyman. But, you know, I have been trained as an actress myself. Male costume is nothing new to me. I often take advantage of the freedom which it gives. I sent John, the coachman, to watch you, ran up-stairs, got into my walking clothes, as I call them, and came down just as you departed.

"Well, I followed you to your door, and so made sure that I was really an object of interest to the celebrated Mr. Sherlock Holmes. Then I, rather imprudently, wished you good-night, and started for the Temple to see my husband.

"We both thought the best resource was flight, when pursued by so formidable an antagonist; so you will find the nest empty when you call to-morrow. As to the photograph, your client may rest in peace. I love and am loved by a better man than he. The King may do what he will without hindrance from one whom he has cruelly wronged. I keep it only to safeguard myself, and to preserve a weapon which will always secure me from any steps which he might take in the future. I leave a photograph which he might care to possess; and I remain, dear Mr. Sherlock Holmes, very truly yours,

"Irene Norton, *née* Adler."

"What a woman — oh, what a woman!" cried

the King of Bohemia, when we had all three read this epistle. "Did I not tell you how quick and resolute she was? Would she not have made an admirable queen? Is it not a pity that she was not on my level?"

"From what I have seen of the lady she seems indeed to be on a very different level to your Majesty," said Holmes, coldly. "I am sorry that I have not been able to bring your Majesty's business to a more successful conclusion."

"On the contrary, my dear sir," cried the King; "nothing could be more successful. I know that her word is inviolate. The photograph is now as safe as if it were in the fire."

"I am glad to hear your Majesty say so."

"I am immensely indebted to you. Pray tell me in what way I can reward you. This ring — " He slipped an emerald snake ring from his finger and held it out upon the palm of his hand.

"Your Majesty has something which I should value even more highly," said Holmes.

"You have but to name it."

"This photograph!"

The King stared at him in amazement.

"Irene's photograph!" he cried. "Certainly, if you wish it."

"I thank your Majesty. Then there is no more to be done in the matter. I have the honour to wish you a very good-morning." He bowed, and, turning away without observing the hand which the King had stretched out to him, he set off in my company for his chambers.

*****

And that was how a great scandal threatened to affect the kingdom of Bohemia, and how the best plans of Mr. Sherlock Holmes were beaten by a woman's wit. He used to make merry over the cleverness of women, but I have not heard him do it of late. And when he speaks of Irene Adler, or when he refers to her photograph, it is always under the honourable title of *the* woman.

VI. The Rope of Fear — Mary E. and Thomas W. Hanshew

If you know anything of the country of Westmoreland, you will know the chief market-town of Merton Sheppard, and if you know Merton Sheppard, you will know there is only one important building in that town besides the massive Town Hall, and that building is the Westmoreland Union Bank — a private concern, well backed by every wealthy magnate in the surrounding district, and patronized by everyone from the highest to the lowest degree.

Anybody will point the building out to you, firstly because of its imposing exterior, and secondly because everyone in the whole county brings his money to Mr. Naylor-Brent, to do with it what he wills. For Mr. Naylor-Brent is the manager, and besides being known far and wide for his integrity, his uprightness of purpose, and his strict sense of justice, he acts to the poorer inhabitants of Merton Sheppard as a sort of father-confessor in all their troubles, both of a social and a financial character.

It was toward the last of September that the big robbery happened, and upon one sunny afternoon at the end of that month Mr. Naylor-Brent was pacing the narrow confines of his handsomely appointed room in the bank, visibly disturbed. That he was awaiting the arrival of someone was evident by his frequent glances at the marble clock which stood upon the mantel-shelf, and which bore across its base a silver plate upon which were inscribed the names of some fifteen or more "grateful customers" whose money had passed successfully through his managerial hands.

At length the door opened, after a discreet knock upon its oaken panels, and an old, bent, and almost decrepit clerk ushered in the portly figure of Mr. Maverick Narkom, Superintendent of Scotland Yard, followed by a heavily-built, dull-looking person in navy blue.

Mr. Naylor-Brent's good-looking, rugged face took on an expression of the keenest relief.

"Mr. Narkom himself! This is indeed more than I expected!" he said with extended hand. "We had the pleasure of meeting once in London, some years ago. Perhaps you have forgotten — ?"

Mr. Narkom's bland face wrinkled into a smile of appreciation.

"Oh no, I haven't," he returned pleasantly, "I remember quite distinctly. I decided to answer your letter in person, and bring with me one of my best men — friend and colleague, you know — Mr. George Headland."

"Pleased to meet you, sir. And if you'll both sit down we can go into the matter at once. That's a comfortable chair over there, Mr. Headland."

They seated themselves, and Mr. Narkom, clearing his throat, proceeded in his usual official manner to "take the floor."

"I understand from headquarters," said he, "that you have had an exceptionally large deposit of banknotes sent up from London for payments in connection with your new canal. Isn't that so, Mr. Brent? I trust the trouble you mentioned in your letter has nothing to do with this money."

Mr. Naylor-Brent's face paled considerably, and his voice had an anxious note in it when he spoke.

"Gad, sir, but it has!" he ejaculated. "That's the trouble itself. Every single banknote is gone. £200,000 is gone and not a trace of it! Heaven only knows what I'm going to do about it, Mr. Narkom, but that's how the matter stands. Every penny is *gone.*"

"Gone!"

Mr. Narkom drew out a red silk handkerchief and wiped his forehead vigorously — a sure sign of nervous excitement — while Mr. Headland exclaimed loudly, "Well, I'm hanged!"

"Someone certainly will be," rapped out Mr. Brent sharply. "For not only have the notes vanished, but I've lost the best night-watchman I ever had, a good, trustworthy man — "

"Lost him?" put in Mr. Headland curiously. "What exactly do you mean by that, Mr. Brent? Did he vanish with the notes?"

"What? Will Simmons? Never in this world! He's not that kind. The man that offered Will Simmons a bribe to betray his trust would answer for it with his life. A more faithful servant, or better fellow never drew breath. No it's dead he is, Mr. Headland, and — I can hardly speak of it yet! I feel so much to blame for putting him on the job at all, but you see we've had a regular series of petty thefts lately; small sums unable to be accounted for, safes opened in the most mysterious manner, and money abstracted — though never any large sums fortunately — even the clerks' coats had not been left untouched. I have had a constant watch kept, but all in vain. So, naturally, when this big deposit came to hand on Tuesday morning, I determined that special precautions should be taken at night, and put poor old Simmons down in the vault with the bank's watchdog for company. That was the last time I saw him alive! He was found writhing in convulsions and by the time that the doctor arrived upon the scene he was dead; the safe was found open, and every note was *gone*!"

"Bad business indeed!" declared Mr. Headland with a shake of the head. "No idea as to the cause of death, Mr. Brent? What was the doctor's verdict?"

Mr. Naylor-Brent's face clouded.

"That's the very dickens of it, he didn't quite know. Said it was evidently a case of poisoning, but was unable to decide further, or to find out what sort of poison — if any — had been used."

"Hmm. I see. And what did the local police say? Have they found any clues yet?"

The manager flushed, and he gave vent to a forced laugh.

"As a matter of fact," he responded, "the local police know nothing about it. I have kept the loss an entire secret until I could call in the help of Scotland Yard."

"A secret, Mr. Brent, with *such* a loss!" ejaculated Mr. Narkom. "That's surely an unusual course to pursue. When a bank loses such a large sum of money, and in banknotes — the most easily handled commodity in the world — and in addition a mysterious murder takes place, one would naturally expect that the first act would be to call in the officers of the law, that is — unless — I see — "

"Well, it's more than I do!" responded Mr. Brent sadly. "Do you see any light, however?"

"Hardly that. But it stands to reason that if you are prepared to make good the loss — a course to which there seems no alternative — there is an obvious possibility that you yourself have some faint idea as to who the criminal is, and are anxious that your suspicions should not be verified."

Mr. Headland (otherwise Cleek) looked at his friend with considerable admiration shining in his eyes. "Beginning to use his old head at last!" he thought as he watched the Superintendent's keen face. "Well, well, it's never too late to mend, anyhow." And then aloud, "Exactly my thought, Mr. Narkom. Perhaps Mr. Brent could enlighten us as to his own suspicions, for I'm positive that he has some tucked away somewhere in his mind."

"Jove, if you're not almost supernatural, Mr. Headland!" returned that gentleman with a heavy sigh. "You have certainly unearthed something which I thought was hidden only in my own soul. That is exactly the reason I have kept silent; my suspicions were I to voice them, might — er — drag the person accused still deeper into the mire of his own foolishness. There's Patterson, for instance, he would arrest him on sight without the slightest compunction."

"Patterson?" threw in Cleek quickly. "Patterson — the name's familiar. Don't suppose though, that it would be the same one — it is a common enough name. Company promoter who made a pile on copper, the first year of the war, and retired with 'the swag' — to put it brutally. 'Tisn't that chap I suppose?"

"The identical man!" returned Mr. Brent, excitedly. "He came here some five years ago, bought up Mount Morris Court — a fine place having a view of the whole town — and he has lately started to run an opposition bank to ours, doing everything in his power to overthrow my position here. It's — it's spite I believe, against myself as well as George. The young fool had the impudence to ask his daughter's hand, and what was more, ran off with her and they were married, which increased Patterson's hatred of us both almost to insanity."

"Hmm. I see," said Cleek. "Who is George?"

"My stepson, Mr. Headland — unfortunately for me — my late wife's boy by her first marriage. I have to admit it regretfully enough, he was the cause of his mother's death. He literally broke her heart by his wild living, and I was only too glad to give him a small allowance — which however helped him with his unhappy marriage — and hoped to see the last of George Barrington."

Cleek twitched up an inquiring eyebrow.

"Unhappy, Mr. Brent?" he queried. "But I understood from you a moment ago it was a love match."

"In the beginning it was purely a question of love, Mr. Headland," responded the manager gravely. "But as you know, when poverty comes in at the door, love sometimes flies out of the window, and from all accounts, the late Miss Patterson never ceases to regret the day she became Mrs. George Barrington. George has been hanging about here this last week or two, and I noticed him trying to renew acquaintance with old Simmons only a day or two ago in the bar of the Rose and Anchor. He — he was also seen prowling round the bank on Tuesday night. So now you know why I was loath to set the ball rolling; old man Patterson would lift the sky to get the chance to have that young waster imprisoned, to say nothing of defaming my personal character at the same time.

"Sooner than that I must endeavour to raise sufficient money by private means to replace the notes — but the death of old Simmons is, of course, another matter. His murderer must and shall be brought to justice, while I have a penny piece in my pocket."

His voice broke suddenly into a harsh sob, and for a moment his hands covered his face. Then he shook himself free of his emotion.

"We will all do our best on that score, Mr. Brent," said Mr. Narkom, after a somewhat lengthy silence. "It is a most unfortunate tragedy indeed, almost a dual one, one might say, but I think you can safely trust yourself in our hands, eh, Headland?"

Cleek bowed his head, while Mr. Brent smiled appreciation of the Superintendent's kindly sympathy.

"I know I can," he said warmly. "Believe me, Mr. Narkom, and you, too, Mr. Headland, I am perfectly content to leave myself with you. But I have my suspicions, and strong ones they are too, and I would not mind laying a bet that Patterson has engineered the whole scheme and is quietly laughing up his sleeve at me."

"That's a bold assertion, Mr. Brent," put in Cleek quietly.

"But justified by facts, Mr. Headland. He has twice tried to bribe Simmons away from me, and last year offered Calcott, my head clerk, a sum of

£5000 to let him have the list of our clients."

"Oho!" said Cleek in two different tones. "One of that sort is he? Not content with a fortune won by profiteering, he must try and ruin others; and having failed to get hold of your list of clients, he tries the bogus theft game, and gambles on that. Hmm! Well, young Barrington may be only a coincidence after all, Mr. Brent. I shouldn't worry too much about him if I were you. Suppose you tell Mr. Narkom and myself the details, right from the beginning, please? When was the murder discovered and who discovered it?"

Mr. Naylor-Brent leaned back in his chair and sighed heavily, as he polished his gold glasses.

"For an affair of such tragic importance, Mr. Headland," he said, "it is singularly lacking in details. There is really nothing more to tell you than that at 6 o'clock, when I myself retired from the bank to my private rooms overhead, I left poor Simmons on guard over the safe; at nine o'clock I was fetched down by the inspector on the beat, who had left young Wilson with the body. After that — "

Cleek lifted a silencing hand.

"One moment," he said. "Who is young Wilson, Mr. Brent, and why should he instead of the inspector have been left alone with the body?"

"Wilson is one of the cashiers, Mr. Headland — a nice lad, but of no particular education. It seems he found the bank's outer door unlatched, and called up the constable on the beat; as luck would have it the inspector happened along, and down they went into the vaults together. But as to why the inspector left young Wilson with the body instead of sending him up for me — well, frankly I had never given the thing a thought until now."

"I see. Funny thing this chap Wilson should have made straight for the vaults though. Did he expect a murder or robbery beforehand? Was he acquainted with the fact that the notes were there, Mr. Brent?"

"No. He knew nothing whatever about them. No one did — that is no one but the head clerk, Mr. Calcott, myself and old Simmons. In bank matters you know the less said about such things the better, and — "

Mr. Narkom nodded.

"Very wise, very wise indeed!" he said, approvingly. "One can't be too careful in money matters, and if I may say so, bank pay being none too high, the temptation must sometimes be rather great. I've a couple of nephews in the bank myself — "

Cleek's eyes suddenly silenced him as though there had been a spoken word.

"This Wilson, Mr. Brent," Cleek asked quietly, "is he a young man?"

"Oh — quite young. Not more than four or five and twenty, I should say. Came from London with an excellent reference, and so far has given every satisfaction. Universal favourite with the firm, and also with old Simmons himself. I believe the two used sometimes to lunch together, and were firm friends. It seems almost a coincidence that the old man should have died in the boy's arms."

"He made no statement, I suppose, before he died, to give an idea of the assassin? But of course you wouldn't know that, as you weren't there."

"As it happens I do, Mr. Headland. Young Wilson, who is frightfully upset — in fact the shock of the thing has completely shattered his nerves, never very strong at the best of times — says that the old man just writhed and writhed, and muttered something about a rope. Then he fell back dead."

"A rope?" said Cleek in surprise. "Was he tied or bound then?"

"That's just it. There was no sign of anything whatever to do with a rope about him. It was possibly a death delusion, or something of the sort. Perhaps the poor old chap was semi-conscious."

"Undoubtedly. And now just one more question, Mr. Brent, before I tire your patience out. We policemen, you know, are terrible nuisances. What time was it when young Wilson discovered the door of the bank unlatched?"

"About half-past nine. I had just noticed my clock striking the half hour, when I was disturbed by the inspector — "

"And wasn't it a bit unusual for a clerk to come back to the bank at that hour — unless he was working overtime?"

Mr. Naylor-Brent's fine head went back with a gesture which conveyed to Cleek the knowledge that he was not in a habit of working any of his employees beyond the given hours.

"He was doing nothing of the sort, Mr. Headland," he responded, a trifle brusquely. "Our firm is particularly keen about the question of working hours. Wilson tells me he came back for his watch which he left behind him, and — "

"And the door was conveniently unlatched and

ready, so he simply fetched in the inspector, and took him straight down into the vaults. Didn't get his watch, I suppose?"

Mr. Naylor-Brent jumped suddenly to his feet, all his self-possession gone for the moment.

"Gad! I never thought of that. Hang it! man, you're making a bigger puzzle of it than ever. You're not insinuating that that boy murdered old Simmons, are you? I can't believe that."

"I'm not insinuating anything," responded Cleek blandly, "but I have to look at things from every angle there is. When you got downstairs with the inspector, Mr. Brent, did you happen to notice the safe or not?"

"Yes, I did. Indeed, I fear that was my first thought — it was natural, with £200,000 Bank of England notes to be responsible for — and at first I thought everything was all right. Then young Wilson told me that he himself had closed the safe door.... What are you smiling at, Mr. Headland? It's no laughing matter, I assure you!"

The queer little one-sided smile, so indicative of the man, travelled for a moment up Cleek's cheek and was gone again in a twinkling.

"Nothing," he responded briefly. "Just a passing thought. Then you mean to say young Wilson closed the safe. Did he know the notes had vanished? But of course you said he knew nothing of them. But if they were there when he looked in — "

His voice trailed off into silence, and he let the rest of the sentence go by default. Mr. Brent's face flushed crimson with excitement.

"Why, at that rate," he ejaculated, "the money

wasn't stolen until young Wilson sent the inspector up for me. And we let him walk quietly out! You were right, Mr. Headland, if I had only done my duty and told Inspector Corkran at once — "

"Steady man, steady. I don't say it *is* so," put in Cleek with a quiet little smile. "I'm only trying to find light — "

"And making it a dashed sight blacker still, begging your pardon," returned Mr. Brent briskly.

"That's as may be. But the devil isn't always as black as he is painted," responded Cleek. "I'd like to see this Wilson, Mr. Brent, unless he is so ill he hasn't been able to attend the office."

"Oh he's back at work to-day, and I'll have him here in a twinkling."

And almost in a twinkling he arrived — a young, slim, pallid youngster, rather given to over-brightness in his choice of ties, and somewhat better dressed than is the lot of most bank clerks. Cleek noted the pearl pin, the well-cut suit he wore, and for a moment his face wore a strange look.

Mr. Naylor-Brent's brisk voice broke the silence.

"These gentlemen are from Scotland Yard, Wilson," he said sharply, "and they want to know just what happened here on Tuesday night. Tell them all you know, please."

Young Wilson's pale face went a queer drab shade like newly baked bread. He began to tremble visibly.

"Happened, sir — happened?" he stammered. "How should I know what happened? I — I only got there just in time and — "

"Yes, yes. We know just when you got there, Mr. Wilson," said Cleek, "but what we want to know is what induced you to go down into the vaults when you fetched the inspector? It seemed a rather unnecessary journey to say the least of it."

"I heard a cry — at least — "

"Right through the closed door of a nine-inch concrete-walled vault, Wilson?" struck in Mr. Brent promptly. "Simmons had been shut in there by myself, Mr. Headland, and — "

"Shut in, Mr. Brent? Shut in, did you say? Then how did Mr. Wilson here, and the inspector enter?"

Young Wilson stretched out his hand imploringly.

"The door was open," he stammered. "I swear it on my honour. And the safe was open, and — and the notes were gone!"

"What notes?" It was Mr. Brent's voice which broke the momentary silence, as he realized the significance of the admission. For answer the young man dropped his face into his shaking hands.

"Oh, the notes — the £200,000! You may think what you like, sir, but I swear I am innocent! I never touched the money, nor did I touch my — Mr. Simmons. I swear it, I swear it!"

"Don't swear too strongly, or you may have to 'un-swear' again," struck in Cleek, severely. "Mr. Narkom and I would like to have a look at the vault itself, and see the body, if you have no objection."

"Certainly. Wilson, you had better come along with us, we might need you. This way, gentlemen."

Speaking, the manager rose to his feet, opened the door of his private office, and proceeded downstairs by way of an equally private staircase to the vaults below. Cleek, Mr. Narkom and young Wilson — very much agitated at the coming ordeal — brought up the rear. As they passed the door leading into the bank, for the use of the clerks, old Calcott came out, and paused respectfully in front of the manager.

"If you excuse me, sir," he said, "I thought perhaps you might like to see this."

He held out a Bank of England £5 note, and Mr. Brent took it and examined it critically. Then a little cry broke from his lips.

"A. 541063!" he exclaimed. "Good Heavens, Calcott, where did this come from? Who — ?"

Calcott rubbed his old hands together as though he were enjoying a tit-bit with much satisfaction.

"Half-an-hour ago, sir, Mr. George Barrington brought it in, and wanted smaller change."

George Barrington! The members of the little party looked at one another in amazement, and Cleek noticed for a moment that young Wilson's tense face relaxed. Mr. George Barrington, eh? The curious little one-sided smile travelled up Cleek's cheek and was gone. The party continued their way downstairs, somewhat silenced by this new development.

A narrow, dark corridor led to the vault itself, which was by no means a large chamber, but remarkable for the extreme solidity of its building. It was concrete, as most vaults are, and lit only by a single electric light, which, when switched on, shone dully against the gray stone walls. The only ventilation it boasted was provided by means of a row of small holes, about an inch in diameter, across one wall — that nearest to the passage — and exactly facing the safe. So small were they that it seemed almost as if not even a mouse could get through one of them, should a mouse be so minded. These holes were placed so low down that it was physically impossible to see through them, and though Cleek's eyes noted their appearance there in the vault, he said nothing and seemed to pay them little attention.

A speedy glance round the room gave him all the details of it! The safe against the wall, the figure of the old bank servant beside it, sleeping his last sleep, and guarding the vault in death as he had not been able to do in life. Cleek crossed toward him, and then stopped suddenly, peering down at what seemed a little twist of paper.

"Hullo!" he said. "Surely you don't allow smoking in the vault, Mr. Brent? Not that it could do much harm but — "

"Certainly not, Mr. Headland," returned the manager warmly. "That is strictly against orders." He glared at young Wilson, who, nervous as he had been before, became obviously more flustered than ever.

"I don't smoke, sir," he stammered in answer to that managerial look of accusation.

"Glad to hear it." Cleek stroked his cigarette case lovingly inside his pocket as though in apology for the libel. "But it's my mistake; not a cigarette end at all, just a twist of paper. Of no account anyway."

He stooped to pick it up, and then giving his hand a flirt, appeared to have tossed it away. Only Mr. Narkom, used to the ways of his famous associate, saw that he had "palmed" it into his pocket. Then Cleek crossed the room and stood a moment looking down at the body, lying there huddled and distorted in the death agony that had so cruelly and mysteriously seized it.

So this was Will Simmons. Well, if the face is any index to the character — which in nine cases out of ten it isn't — then Mr. Naylor-Brent's confidence had certainly not been misplaced. A fine, clean, rugged face this, with set lips, a face that would never fail a friend, and never forgive an enemy. Young Wilson, who had stepped up beside Cleek, shivered suddenly as he looked down at the body, and closed his eyes.

Mr. Brent's voice broke the silence that the sight of death so often brings.

"I think," he said quietly, "if you don't mind, gentlemen, I'll get back to my office. There are important matters at stake just now, so if you'll excuse me — It's near closing time you know, and there are many important matters to see to. Wilson, you stay here with these gentlemen, and render any assistance that you can. Show them round if they wish it. You need not resume work to-day. Anything which you wish to know, please call upon me."

"Thanks. We'll remember," Cleek bowed ceremoniously, as the manager retreated, "but no doubt Mr. Wilson here will give us all the assistance we require, Mr. Brent. We'll make an examination of the body first, and let you know the verdict."

The door closed on Mr. Brent's figure, and

Cleek and Mr. Narkom and young Wilson were alone with the dead.

Cleek went down upon his knees before the still figure, and examined it from end to end. The clenched hands were put to the keenest scrutiny, but he passed no comment, only glancing now and again from those same hands to the figure of the young cashier who stood trembling beside him.

"Hmm, convulsions," he finally said softly to himself, and Mr. Narkom watched his face with intense eagerness. "Might be aconite — but how administered?" Again he stood silent, his brain moving swiftly down an avenue of thought, and if the thoughts could have been seen, they should have shown something like this: Convulsions — writhing — twisting — tied up in knots of pain — a *rope*.

Suddenly he wheeled swiftly upon Wilson, his face a mask for his emotions.

"Look here," he said sternly, "I want you to tell me the exact truth, Mr. Wilson. It's the wisest way when dealing with the police, you know. Are you positively certain Simmons said nothing as to the cause of his death? What exactly were his last words to you?"

"I begged him to tell me who it was who had injured him," replied Wilson, in a shaking voice, "but all he could say was, 'The rope — mind the Rope — the Rope of Fear — the Rope of Fear,' and then he was gone. But there was no sign of any rope, Mr. Headland, and I can't imagine what the dear old man was driving at. And now to think he is dead — dead — "

His voice broke and was silent for a moment.

Once again Cleek spoke.

"And you saw nothing, heard nothing?"

"Well — I hardly know. There was a sound — a faint whisper, reedlike and thin, almost like a long drawn sigh. I really thought I must have imagined it, and when I listened again it had gone. After that I rushed to the safe and — "

"Why did you do that?"

"Because he had told me at dinner-time about the notes, and made me promise I wouldn't mention it, and I was afraid someone had stolen them."

"Is it likely that anyone overheard your conversation then? Where were you lunching?"

"In the Rose and Crown," Wilson's voice trembled again as though the actual recalling of the thing terrified him anew. "Simmons and I often had lunch together. There was no one else at our table, and the place was practically empty. The only person near was old Ramagee, the black chap who keeps the Indian bazaar in the town. He's an old inhabitant, but even now hardly understands English, and most of the time he's so drugged with opium, that if did hear he'd never understand. He was certainly blind to the world that lunch time, because my — my friend, Simmons, I mean, noticed it."

"Indeed!" Cleek stroked his chin thoughtfully for some moments. Then he sniffed the air, and uttered a casual remark: "Fond of sweets still, are you Mr. Wilson? Peppermint drops, or aniseed balls, eh?"

Mr. Narkom's eyes fairly bulged with amazement, and young Wilson flushed angrily.

"I am not such a fool as all that, Mr. Headland," he said quickly. "If I don't smoke, I certainly don't go about sucking candy like a kid. I never cared for 'em as a youngster, and I haven't had any for a cat's age. What made you ask?"

"Nothing, simply my fancy." But, nevertheless, Cleek continued to sniff, and then suddenly with a little excited sound went down on his hands and knees and began examining the stone floor.

"It's not possible — and yet — and yet, I must be right," he said softly, getting to his feet at last. "'A rope of fear' was what he said, wasn't it? 'A rope of fear.'" He crossed suddenly to the safe, and bending over it, examined the handle and doors critically. And at the moment Mr. Brent reappeared. Cleek switched round upon his heel, and smiled across at him.

"Able to spare us a little more of your valuable time, Mr. Brent?" he said politely. "Well, I was just coming up. There's nothing really to be gained here. I have been looking over the safe for finger-prints, and there's not much doubt about whose they are. Mr. Wilson here had better come upstairs and tell us just exactly what he did with the notes, and — "

Young Wilson's face went suddenly gray. He clenched his hands together and breathed hard like a spent runner.

"I tell you, they were gone," he cried desperately. "They were gone. I looked for them, and didn't find them. They were gone — gone — gone!"

But Cleek seemed not to take the slightest notice of him, and swinging upon his heel followed in the wake of the manager's broad back, while Wilson perforce had to return with Mr. Narkom. Half way up the stairs, however, Cleek suddenly stopped, and gave vent to a hurried ejaculation.

"Silly idiot that I am!" he said crossly. "I have left my magnifying glass on top of the safe — and it's the most necessary tool we policemen have. Don't bother to come, Mr. Brent, if you'll just lend me the keys of the vault. Thanks, I'll be right back."

It was certainly not much more than a moment when he did return, and the other members of the little party had barely reached the private office when he fairly rushed in after them. There was a look of supreme satisfaction in his eyes.

"Here it is," he said, lifting the glass up for all to see. "And look here, Mr. Brent, I've changed my mind about discussing the matter any further here. The best thing you can do is to go down in a cab with Mr. Narkom to the police station, and get a warrant for this young man's arrest — no, don't speak, Mr. Wilson, I've not finished yet — and take him along with you. I will stay here and just scribble down the facts. It'll save no end of bother, and we can take our man straight up to London with us, under proper arrest. I shan't be more than ten minutes at the most."

Mr. Brent nodded assent.

"As you please, Mr. Headland," he said gravely. "We'll go along at once. Wilson, you understand you are to come with us? It's no use trying to get away from it, man, you're up against it now. You'd better just keep a stiff upper lip and face the music. I'm ready, Mr. Narkom."

Quietly they took their departure, in a hastily found cab, leaving Cleek, the picture of stolid policemanism, with notebook and pencil in hand, busily inscribing what he was pleased to call "the facts."

Only "ten minutes" Cleek had asked for, but it was nearer twenty before he was ushered out of the side entrance of the bank by the old housekeeper, and though perhaps it was only sheer luck that caused him to nearly tumble into the arms of Mr. George Barrington — whom he recognized from the word picture of that gentleman given by Mr. Brent some time before — it was decidedly by arrangement that, after a few careless words on the part of Cleek, Barrington, his face blank with astonishment, accompanied this stranger down to the police station.

They found a grim little party awaiting them but at sight of Cleek's face Mr. Narkom started forward, and put a hand upon his friend's arm.

"What have you found, Headland?" he asked excitedly.

"Just what I expected to find," came the triumphant reply. "Now, Mr. Wilson, you are going to hear the end of the story. Do you want to see what I found, gentlemen? Here it is." He fumbled in his big coat pocket for a moment and pulled out a parcel which crackled crisply. "The notes!"

"Good God!"

It was young Wilson who spoke.

"Yes, a *very* good God — even to sinners, Mr. Wilson. We don't always deserve all the goodness we get, you know," Cleek went on. "The notes are found you see; the notes, you murderer, you despicable thief, the notes which were entrusted to your care by the innocent people who pinned their faith to you."

Speaking, he leaped forward, past the waiting inspector and Mr. Narkom, past the shabby, down-at-heel figure of George Barrington, past the slim, shaking Wilson, and straight at the substantial figure of Mr. Naylor-Brent, as he stood leaning with one arm upon the inspector's high desk.

So surprising, so unexpected was the attack, that this victim was overpowered and the bracelets snapped upon his wrists before anyone present had begun to realize exactly what had happened.

Then Cleek rose to his feet.

"What's that, Inspector?" he said in answer to a hurriedly spoken query. "A mistake? Oh dear, no. No mistake whatever. Our friend here understands that quite well. Thought you'd have escaped with that £200,000 and left your confederate to bear the brunt of the whole thing, did you? Or else young Wilson here whom you'd so terrorized! A very pretty plot indeed, only Hamilton Cleek happened to come along instead of Mr. George Headland, and show you a thing or two about plots."

"Hamilton Cleek!" The name fell from every pair of lips, and even Brent himself stared at this wizard whom all the world knew, and who unfortunately had crossed his path when he least wanted him.

"Yes, Hamilton Cleek, gentlemen. Cleek of Scotland Yard. And a very good thing for you, Mr. Wilson, that I happened to come along. Things looked very black for you, you know, and those beastly nerves of yours made it worse. And if it hadn't been for this cad's confederate — "

"Confederate, Mr. Cleek?" put in Wilson shakily. "I — I don't understand. Who could have been his confederate?"

"None other than old Ramagee," responded Cleek. "You'll find him drugged as usual, in the Rose and Crown. I've seen him there only a while ago. But now he is minus a constant companion of his.... And here is the actual murderer."

He put his hand into another capacious pocket and drew forth a smallish, glass box.

"The Rope of Fear, gentlemen," he said quietly, "a vicious little rattler of the most deadly sort. And it won't be long before that gentleman there becomes acquainted with another sort of rope. Take him away, Inspector. The bare sight of him hurts an honest man's eyes."

And they took him away forthwith, a writhing, furious Thing, utterly transformed from the genial personality which had for so long swindled and outwitted a trusting public.

As the door closed upon them, Cleek turned to young Wilson and held out his hand.

"I'm sorry to have accused you as I did," he said softly, with a little smile, "but that is a policeman's way, you know. Strategy is part of the game — though it was a poor trick of mine to cause you additional pain. You must forgive me. I don't doubt the death of your father was a great shock, although you tried manfully to conceal the relationship. No doubt it was his wish — not yours."

A sudden transformation came over Wilson's pale, haggard face. It was like the sun shining after a heavy storm.

"You — knew?" he said, over and over again. "You *knew*? Oh, Mr. Cleek, now I can speak out at last. Father always made me promise to be silent, he — he wanted me to be a gentleman, and he'd spent every penny he possessed to get me well enough educated to enter the bank. He was mad for money, mad for anything which was going to better my position. And — and I was afraid when he told me about the notes, he might be tempted — Oh! It was dreadful of me, I know, to think of it, but I knew he doted upon me, I was afraid he might try and take one or two of them, hoping they wouldn't be missed out of so great an amount. You see we'd been in money difficulties and were still paying my college fees off after all this time. So I went back to keep watch with him — and found him dying — though how you *knew* — "

His voice trailed off into silence, and Cleek smiled kindly.

"By the identical shape of your hands, my boy. I never saw two pairs of hands so much alike in all my life. And then your agitation made me risk the guess.... What's that, Inspector? How was the murder committed, and what did this little rattler have to do with it? Well, quite simple. The snake was put in the safe with the notes, and a trail of aniseed — of which snakes are very fond, you know — laid from there to the foot of old Simmons. The safe door was left ajar — though in the half dusk the old man certainly never noticed it. I found all this out from those few words of Wilson's about 'the rope,' and from his having heard a reed-like sound. I had to do some hard thinking, I can tell you. When I went downstairs again, Mr. Narkom, after my magnifying glass, I turned down poor Simmons's sock and found the mark I expected — the snake had crawled up his leg and struck home.

"Why did I suspect Mr. Brent? Well, it was obvious almost from the very first, for he was so anxious to throw suspicion upon Mr. Barrington here, and Wilson — with Patterson thrown in for good measure. Then again it was certain that no one else would have been allowed into the vault by Simmons, much less to go to the safe itself, and open it with the keys. That he did go to the safe was apparent by the finger prints upon it, and as they too smelt of aniseed, the whole thing began to look decidedly funny. The trail of aniseed led straight up to where Simmons lay, so I can only suppose that after Brent released the snake — the trail of course having been laid beforehand, when he was alone — Brent must have stood and waited until he saw it actually strike, and — How do I know that, Mr. Wilson? Well, he smoked a cigarette there, anyhow. The stub I found bore the same name as those in his box, and it was smoked identically the same way as a couple which lay in his ashtray.

"I could only conclude that he was waiting for something to happen, and as the snake struck, he grabbed up the bundle of notes, quite forgetting to close the safe-door, and rushed out of the vault. Ramagee was in the corridor outside, and probably whistled the snake back through the ventilating holes near the floor, instead of venturing near the body himself. You remember, you heard the sound of that pipe, Mr. Wilson? Ramagee probably made his escape while the Inspector was upstairs. Unfortunately for him, he ran right into Mr. George Barrington here, and when, as he tells me, he later told Brent about seeing Ramagee, well, the whole thing became as plain as a pikestaff."

"Yes," put in George Barrington, excitedly, taking up the tale in his weak, rather silly voice, "my step-father refused to believe me, and gave me £20 in notes to go away. I suppose he didn't notice they were some of the stolen ones. I changed one of them at the bank this morning, but I had no idea how important they were until I knocked into Mr. — Mr. Cleek here. And he made me come along with him."

Mr. Narkom looked at Cleek, and Cleek looked at Mr. Narkom, and the blank wonder in the Superintendent's eyes caused him to smile.

"Another feather in the cap of foolish old Scotland Yard, isn't it?" he said. "Time we made tracks I think. Coming our way, Mr. Wilson? We'll see you back home if you like. You're too upset to go on alone. Good afternoon, Inspector and — good-bye. I'll leave the case with you. It's safe enough in your hands, but if you take my tip you'll put that human beast in as tight a lock-up as the station affords."

Then he linked one arm in Mr. Narkom's and the other arm in that of the admiring, and wholly speechless Wilson, and went out into the sunshine.

VII. The Safety Match — Anton Chekhov

I

On the morning of October 6, 1885, in the office of the Inspector of Police of the second division of S — District, there appeared a respectably dressed young man, who announced that his master, Marcus Ivanovitch Klausoff, a retired officer of the Horse Guards, separated from his wife, had been murdered. While making this announcement the young man was white and terribly agitated. His hands trembled and his eyes were full of terror.

"Whom have I the honour of addressing?" asked the inspector.

"Psyekoff, Lieutenant Klausoff's agent; agriculturist and mechanician!"

The inspector and his deputy, on visiting the scene of the occurrence in company with Psyekoff, found the following: Near the wing in which Klausoff had lived was gathered a dense crowd. The news of the murder had sped swift as lightning through the neighbourhood, and the peasantry, thanks to the fact that the day was a holiday, had hurried together from all the neighbouring villages. There was much commotion and talk. Here and there, pale, tear-stained faces were seen. The door of Klausoff's bedroom was found locked. The key was inside.

"It is quite clear that the scoundrels got in by the window!" said Psyekoff as they examined the door.

They went to the garden, into which the bedroom window opened. The window looked dark and ominous. It was covered by a faded green curtain. One corner of the curtain was slightly turned up, which made it possible to look into the bedroom.

"Did any of you look into the window?" asked the inspector.

"Certainly not, your worship!" answered Ephraim, the gardener, a little gray-haired old man, who looked like a retired sergeant. "Who's going to look in, if all their bones are shaking?"

"Ah, Marcus Ivanovitch, Marcus Ivanovitch!" sighed the inspector, looking at the window, "I told you you would come to a bad end! I told the dear man, but he wouldn't listen! Dissipation doesn't bring any good!"

"Thanks to Ephraim," said Psyekoff; "but for him, we would never have guessed. He was the first to guess that something was wrong. He comes to me this morning, and says: 'Why is the master so long getting up? He hasn't left his bedroom for a whole week!' The moment he said that, it was just as if someone had hit me with an axe. The thought flashed through my mind, 'We haven't had a sight of him since last Saturday, and to-day is Sunday'! Seven whole days — not a doubt of it!"

"Ay, poor fellow!" again sighed the inspector. "He was a clever fellow, finely educated, and kind-hearted at that! And in society, nobody could touch him! But he was a waster, God rest his soul! I was prepared for anything since he refused to live with Olga Petrovna. Poor thing, a good wife, but a sharp tongue! Stephen!" the inspector called to one of his deputies, "go over to my house this minute, and send Andrew to the captain to lodge an information with him! Tell him that Marcus Ivanovitch has been murdered. And run over to the orderly; why should he sit there, kicking his heels? Let him come here! And go as fast as you can to the examining magistrate, Nicholas Yermolaïyevitch. Tell him to come over here! Wait; I'll write him a note!"

The inspector posted sentinels around the wing, wrote a letter to the examining magistrate, and then went over to the director's for a glass of tea. Ten minutes later he was sitting on a stool, carefully nibbling a lump of sugar, and swallowing the scalding tea.

"There you are!" he was saying to Psyekoff; "there you are! A noble by birth! a rich man — a favourite of the gods, you may say, as Pushkin has it, and what did he come to? He drank and dissipated and — there you are — he's murdered."

After a couple of hours the examining magistrate drove up. Nicholas Yermolaïyevitch Chubikoff — for that was the magistrate's name — was a tall, fleshy old man of sixty, who had been wrestling with the duties of his office for a quarter of a century. Everybody in the district knew him as an honest man, wise, energetic, and in love with his work. He was accompanied to the scene of the murder by his inveterate companion, fellow worker, and secretary, Dukovski, a tall young fellow of twenty-six.

"Is it possible, gentlemen?" cried Chubikoff, entering Psyekoff's room, and quickly shaking hands with everyone. "Is it possible? Marcus Ivanovitch? Murdered? No! It is impossible! Im-poss-i-ble!"

"Go in there!" sighed the inspector.

"Lord, have mercy on us! Only last Friday I saw him at the fair in Farabankoff. I had a drink of vodka with him, save the mark!"

"Go in there!" again sighed the inspector.

They sighed, uttered exclamations of horror, drank a glass of tea each, and went to the wing.

"Get back!" the orderly cried to the peasants.

Going to the wing, the examining magistrate began his work by examining the bedroom door. The door proved to be of pine, painted yellow, and was uninjured. Nothing was found which could serve as a clew. They had to break in the door.

"Everyone not here on business is requested to keep away!" said the magistrate, when, after much hammering and shaking, the door yielded to axe and chisel. "I request this, in the interest of the investigation. Orderly, don't let anyone in!"

Chubikoff, his assistant, and the inspector opened the door, and hesitatingly, one after the other, entered the room. Their eyes met the following sight: Beside the single window stood the big wooden bed with a huge feather mattress. On the crumpled feather bed lay a tumbled, crumpled quilt. The pillow, in a cotton pillow-case, also much crumpled, was dragging on the floor. On the table beside the bed lay a silver watch and a silver twenty-kopeck piece. Beside them lay some sulphur matches. Beside the bed, the little table, and the single chair, there was no furniture in the room. Looking under the bed, the inspector saw a couple of dozen empty bottles, an old straw hat, and a quart of vodka. Under the table lay one top boot, covered with dust. Casting a glance around the room, the magistrate frowned and grew red in the face.

"Scoundrels!" he muttered, clenching his fists.

"And where is Marcus Ivanovitch?" asked Dukovski in a low voice.

"Mind your own business!" Chubikoff answered roughly. "Be good enough to examine the floor! This is not the first case of the kind I have had to deal with! Eugraph Kuzmitch," he said, turning to the inspector, and lowering his voice, "in 1870 I had another case like this. But you must remember it — the murder of the merchant Portraitoff. It was just the same there. The scoundrels murdered him, and dragged the corpse out through the window — "

Chubikoff went up to the window, pulled the curtain to one side, and carefully pushed the window. The window opened.

"It opens, you see! It wasn't fastened. Hm! There are tracks under the window. Look! There is the track of a knee! Somebody got in there. We must examine the window thoroughly."

"There is nothing special to be found on the floor," said Dukovski. "No stains or scratches. The only thing I found was a struck safety match. Here it is! So far as I remember, Marcus Ivanovitch did not smoke. And he always used sulphur matches, never safety matches. Perhaps this safety match may serve as a clew!"

"Oh, do shut up!" cried the magistrate deprecatingly. "You go on about your match! I can't abide these dreamers! Instead of chasing matches, you had better examine the bed!"

After a thorough examination of the bed, Dukovski reported:

"There are no spots, either of blood or of anything else. There are likewise no new torn places.

On the pillow there are signs of teeth. The quilt is stained with something which looks like beer and smells like beer. The general aspect of the bed gives grounds for thinking that a struggle took place on it."

"I know there was a struggle, without your telling me! You are not being asked about a struggle. Instead of looking for struggles, you had better — "

"Here is one top boot, but there is no sign of the other."

"Well, and what of that?"

"It proves that they strangled him, while he was taking his boots off. He hadn't time to take the second boot off when — "

"There you go! — and how do you know they strangled him?"

"There are marks of teeth on the pillow. The pillow itself is badly crumpled, and thrown a couple of yards from the bed."

"Listen to his foolishness! Better come into the garden. You would be better employed examining the garden than digging around here. I can do that without you!"

When they reached the garden they began by examining the grass. The grass under the window was crushed and trampled. A bushy burdock growing under the window close to the wall was also trampled. Dukovski succeeded in finding on it some broken twigs and a piece of cotton wool. On the upper branches were found some fine hairs of dark blue wool.

"What colour was his last suit?" Dukovski

asked Psyekoff.

"Yellow crash."

"Excellent! You see they wore blue!"

A few twigs of the burdock were cut off, and carefully wrapped in paper by the investigators. At this point Police Captain Artsuybasheff Svistakovski and Dr. Tyutyeff arrived. The captain bade them "Good day!" and immediately began to satisfy his curiosity. The doctor, a tall, very lean man, with dull eyes, a long nose, and a pointed chin, without greeting anyone or asking about anything, sat down on a log, sighed, and began:

"The Servians are at war again! What in heaven's name can they want now? Austria, it's all your doing!"

The examination of the window from the outside did not supply any conclusive data. The examination of the grass and the bushes nearest to the window yielded a series of useful clews. For example, Dukovski succeeded in discovering a long, dark streak, made up of spots, on the grass, which led some distance into the centre of the garden. The streak ended under one of the lilac bushes in a dark brown stain. Under this same lilac bush was found a top boot, which turned out to be the fellow of the boot already found in the bedroom.

"That is a blood stain made some time ago," said Dukovski, examining the spot.

At the word "blood" the doctor rose, and going over lazily, looked at the spot.

"Yes, it is blood!" he muttered.

"That shows he wasn't strangled, if there was

blood," said Chubikoff, looking sarcastically at Dukovski.

"They strangled him in the bedroom; and here, fearing he might come round again, they struck him a blow with some sharp-pointed instrument. The stain under the bush proves that he lay there a considerable time, while they were looking about for some way of carrying him out of the garden."

"Well, and how about the boot?"

"The boot confirms completely my idea that they murdered him while he was taking his boots off before going to bed. He had already taken off one boot, and the other, this one here, he had only had time to take half off. The half-off boot came off of itself, while the body was dragged over, and fell — "

"There's a lively imagination for you!" laughed Chubikoff. "He goes on and on like that! When will you learn enough to drop your deductions? Instead of arguing and deducing, it would be much better if you took some of the blood-stained grass for analysis!"

When they had finished their examination, and drawn a plan of the locality, the investigators went to the director's office to write their report and have breakfast. While they were breakfasting they went on talking:

"The watch, the money, and so on — all untouched — " Chubikoff began, leading off the talk, "show as clearly as that two and two are four that the murder was not committed for the purpose of robbery."

"The murder was committed by an educated

man!" insisted Dukovski.

"What evidence have you of that?"

"The safety match proves that to me, for the peasants hereabouts are not yet acquainted with safety matches. Only the landowners use them, and by no means all of them. And it is evident that there was not one murderer, but at least three. Two held him, while one killed him. Klausoff was strong, and the murderers must have known it!"

"What good would his strength be, supposing he was asleep?"

"The murderers came on him while he was taking off his boots. If he was taking off his boots, that proves that he wasn't asleep!"

"Stop inventing your deductions! Better eat!"

"In my opinion, your worship," said the gardener Ephraim, setting the samovar on the table, "it was nobody but Nicholas who did this dirty trick!"

"Quite possible," said Psyekoff.

"And who is Nicholas?"

"The master's valet, your worship," answered Ephraim. "Who else could it be? He's a rascal, your worship! He's a drunkard and a blackguard, the like of which Heaven should not permit! He always took the master his vodka and put the master to bed. Who else could it be? And I also venture to point out to your worship, he once boasted at the public house that he would kill the master! It happened on account of Aquilina, the woman, you know. He was making up to a soldier's widow. She pleased the master; the master made friends with her himself, and Nicholas — naturally, he was mad! He is rolling about drunk in the kitchen now. He is crying, and telling lies, saying he is sorry for the master — "

The examining magistrate ordered Nicholas to be brought. Nicholas, a lanky young fellow, with a long, freckled nose, narrow-chested, and wearing an old jacket of his master's, entered Psyekoff's room, and bowed low before the magistrate. His face was sleepy and tear-stained. He was tipsy and could hardly keep his feet.

"Where is your master?" Chubikoff asked him.

"Murdered! your worship!"

As he said this, Nicholas blinked and began to weep.

"We know he was murdered. But where is he now? Where is his body?"

"They say he was dragged out of the window and buried in the garden!"

"Hum! The results of the investigation are known in the kitchen already! — That's bad! Where were you, my good fellow, the night the master was murdered? Saturday night, that is."

Nicholas raised his head, stretched his neck, and began to think.

"I don't know, your worship," he said. "I was drunk and don't remember."

"An alibi!" whispered Dukovski, smiling, and rubbing his hands.

"So-o! And why is there blood under the master's window?"

Nicholas jerked his head up and considered.

"Hurry up!" said the Captain of Police.

"Right away! That blood doesn't amount to anything, your worship! I was cutting a chicken's throat. I was doing it quite simply, in the usual way, when all of a sudden it broke away and started to run. That is where the blood came from."

Ephraim declared that Nicholas did kill a chicken every evening, and always in some new place, but that nobody ever heard of a half-killed chicken running about the garden, though of course it wasn't impossible.

"An alibi," sneered Dukovski; "and what an asinine alibi!"

"Did you know Aquilina?"

"Yes, your worship, I know her."

"And the master cut you out with her?"

"Not at all. *He* cut me out — Mr. Psyekoff there, Ivan Mikhailovitch; and the master cut Ivan Mikhailovitch out. That is how it was."

Psyekoff grew confused and began to scratch his left eye. Dukovski looked at him attentively, noted his confusion, and started. He noticed that the director had dark blue trousers, which he had not observed before. The trousers reminded him of the dark blue threads found on the burdock. Chubikoff in his turn glanced suspiciously at Psyekoff.

"Go!" he said to Nicholas. "And now permit me to put a question to you, Mr. Psyekoff. Of course you were here last Saturday evening?"

"Yes! I had supper with Marcus Ivanovitch about ten o'clock."

"And afterward?"

"Afterward — afterward — Really, I do not remember," stammered Psyekoff. "I had a good deal to drink at supper. I don't remember when or where I went to sleep. Why are you all looking at me like that, as if I was the murderer?"

"Where were you when you woke up?"

"I was in the servants' kitchen, lying behind the stove! They can all confirm it. How I got behind the stove I don't know — "

"Do not get agitated. Did you know Aquilina?"

"There's nothing extraordinary about that — "

"She first liked you and then preferred Klausoff?"

"Yes. Ephraim, give us some more mushrooms! Do you want some more tea, Eugraph Kuzmitch?"

A heavy, oppressive silence began and lasted fully five minutes. Dukovski silently kept his piercing eyes fixed on Psyekoff's pale face. The silence was finally broken by the examining magistrate:

"We must go to the house and talk with Maria Ivanovna, the sister of the deceased. Perhaps she may be able to supply some clews."

Chubikoff and his assistant expressed their thanks for the breakfast, and went toward the house. They found Klausoff's sister, Maria Ivanovna, an old maid of forty-five, at prayer before the big case of family icons. When she saw the portfolios in her guests' hands, and their official caps, she grew pale.

"Let me begin by apologizing for disturbing, so

to speak, your devotions," began the gallant Chubikoff, bowing and scraping. "We have come to you with a request. Of course, you have heard already. There is a suspicion that your dear brother, in some way or other, has been murdered. The will of God, you know. No one can escape death, neither czar nor ploughman. Could you not help us with some clew, some explanation — ?"

"Oh, don't ask me!" said Maria Ivanovna, growing still paler, and covering her face with her hands. "I can tell you nothing. Nothing! I beg you! I know nothing — What can I do? Oh, no! no! — not a word about my brother! If I die, I won't say anything!"

Maria Ivanovna began to weep, and left the room. The investigators looked at each other, shrugged their shoulders, and beat a retreat.

"Confound the woman!" scolded Dukovski, going out of the house. "It is clear she knows something, and is concealing it! And the chambermaid has a queer expression too! Wait, you wretches! We'll ferret it all out!"

In the evening Chubikoff and his deputy, lit on their road by the pale moon, wended their way homeward. They sat in their carriage and thought over the results of the day. Both were tired and kept silent. Chubikoff was always unwilling to talk while travelling, and the talkative Dukovski remained silent, to fall in with the elder man's humour. But at the end of their journey the deputy could hold in no longer, and said:

"It is quite certain," he said, "that Nicholas had something to do with the matter. *Non dubitandum est!* You can see by his face what sort of a case he is! His alibi betrays him, body and bones. But it is also certain that he did not set the thing going. He was only the stupid hired tool. You agree? And the humble Psyekoff was not without some slight share in the matter. His dark blue breeches, his agitation, his lying behind the stove in terror after the murder, his alibi and — Aquilina — "

"'Grind away, Emilian; it's your week!' So, according to you, whoever knew Aquilina is the murderer! Hothead! You ought to be sucking a bottle, and not handling affairs! You were one of Aquilina's admirers yourself — does it follow that you are implicated too?"

"Aquilina was cook in your house for a month. I am saying nothing about that! The night before that Saturday I was playing cards with you, and saw you, otherwise I should be after you too! It isn't the woman that matters, old chap! It is the mean, nasty, low spirit of jealousy that matters. The retiring young man was not pleased when they got the better of him, you see! His vanity, don't you see? He wanted revenge. Then, those thick lips of his suggest passion. So there you have it: wounded self-love and passion. That is quite enough motive for a murder. We have two of them in our hands; but who is the third? Nicholas and Psyekoff held him, but who smothered him? Psyekoff is shy, timid, an all-round coward. And Nicholas would not know how to smother with a pillow. His sort use an axe or a club. Some third person did the smothering; but who was it?"

Dukovski crammed his hat down over his eyes and pondered. He remained silent until the carriage rolled up to the magistrate's door.

"Eureka!" he said, entering the little house and throwing off his overcoat. "Eureka, Nicholas Yermolaïyevitch! The only thing I can't understand is, how it did not occur to me sooner! Do you know who the third person was?"

"Oh, for goodness sake, shut up! There is supper! Sit down to your evening meal!"

The magistrate and Dukovski sat down to supper. Dukovski poured himself out a glass of vodka, rose, drew himself up, and said, with sparkling eyes:

"Well, learn that the third person, who acted in concert with that scoundrel Psyekoff, and did the smothering, was a woman! Yes-s! I mean — the murdered man's sister, Maria Ivanovna!"

Chubikoff choked over his vodka, and fixed his eyes on Dukovski.

"You aren't — what's-its-name? Your head isn't what-do-you-call-it? You haven't a pain in it?"

"I am perfectly well! Very well, let us say that I am crazy; but how do you explain her confusion when we appeared? How do you explain her unwillingness to give us any information? Let us admit that these are trifles. Very well! All right! But remember their relations. She detested her brother. She never forgave him for living apart from his wife. She of the Old Faith, while in her eyes he is a godless profligate. There is where the germ of her hate was hatched. They say he succeeded in making her believe that he was an angel of Satan. He even went in for spiritualism in her presence!"

"Well, what of that?"

"You don't understand? She, as a member of the Old Faith, murdered him through fanaticism. It was not only that she was putting to death a weed, a profligate — she was freeing the world of an antichrist! — and there, in her opinion, was her service, her religious achievement! Oh, you don't know those old maids of the Old Faith. Read Dostoyevsky! And what does Lyeskoff say about them, or Petcherski? It was she, and nobody else, even if you cut me open. She smothered him! O treacherous woman! wasn't that the reason why she was kneeling before the icons, when we came in, just to take our attention away? 'Let me kneel down and pray,' she said to herself, 'and they will think I am tranquil and did not expect them!' That is the plan of all novices in crime, Nicholas Yermolaïyevitch, old pal! My dear old man, won't you intrust this business to me? Let me personally bring it through! Friend, I began it and I will finish it!"

Chubikoff shook his head and frowned.

"We know how to manage difficult matters ourselves," he said; "and your business is not to push yourself in where you don't belong. Write from dictation when you are dictated to; that is your job!"

Dukovski flared up, banged the door, and disappeared.

"Clever rascal!" muttered Chubikoff, glancing after him. "Awfully clever! But too much of a hothead. I must buy him a cigar case at the fair as a present."

The next day, early in the morning, a young man with a big head and a pursed-up mouth, who came from Klausoff's place, was introduced to the magistrate's office. He said he was the shepherd Daniel, and brought a very interesting piece of information.

"I was a bit drunk," he said. "I was with my pal till midnight. On my way home, as I was drunk, I went into the river for a bath. I was taking a bath, when I looked up. Two men were walking along the dam, carrying something black. 'Shoo!' I cried at them. They got scared, and went off like the wind toward Makareff's cabbage garden. Strike me dead, if they weren't carrying away the master!"

That same day, toward evening, Psyekoff and Nicholas were arrested and brought under guard to the district town. In the town they were committed to the cells of the prison.

II

A fortnight passed.

It was morning. The magistrate Nicholas Yermolaïyevitch was sitting in his office before a green table, turning over the papers of the "Klausoff case"; Dukovski was striding restlessly up and down like a wolf in a cage.

"You are convinced of the guilt of Nicholas and Psyekoff," he said, nervously plucking at his young beard. "Why will you not believe in the guilt of Maria Ivanovna? Are there not proofs enough for you?"

"I don't say I am not convinced. I am convinced, but somehow I don't believe it! There are no real proofs, but just a kind of philosophizing — fanaticism, this and that — "

"You can't do without an axe and bloodstained sheets. Those jurists! Very well, I'll prove it to you! You will stop sneering at the psychological side of the affair! To Siberia with your Maria Ivanovna! I will prove it! If philosophy is not enough for you, I have something substantial for you. It will show you how correct my philosophy is. Just give me permission — "

"What are you going on about?"

"About the safety match! Have you forgotten it? I haven't! I am going to find out who struck it in the murdered man's room. It was not Nicholas that struck it; it was not Psyekoff, for neither of them had any matches when they were examined; it was the third person, Maria Ivanovna. I will prove it to you. Just give me permission to go through the district to find out."

"That's enough! Sit down. Let us go on with the examination."

Dukovski sat down at a little table, and plunged his long nose in a bundle of papers.

"Bring in Nicholas Tetekhoff!" cried the examining magistrate.

They brought Nicholas in. Nicholas was pale and thin as a rail. He was trembling.

"Tetekhoff!" began Chubikoff. "In 1879 you were tried in the Court of the First Division, convicted of theft, and sentenced to imprisonment. In 1882 you were tried a second time for theft, and were again imprisoned. We know all — "

Astonishment was depicted on Nicholas's face. The examining magistrate's omniscience startled him. But soon his expression of astonishment changed to extreme indignation. He began to cry and requested permission to go and wash his face and quiet down. They led him away.

"Bring in Psyekoff!" ordered the examining

magistrate.

They brought in Psyekoff. The young man had changed greatly during the last few days. He had grown thin and pale, and looked haggard. His eyes had an apathetic expression.

"Sit down, Psyekoff," said Chubikoff. "I hope that to-day you are going to be reasonable, and will not tell lies, as you did before. All these days you have denied that you had anything to do with the murder of Klausoff, in spite of all the proofs that testify against you. That is foolish. Confession will lighten your guilt. This is the last time I am going to talk to you. If you do not confess to-day, to-morrow it will be too late. Come, tell me all — "

"I know nothing about it. I know nothing about your proofs," answered Psyekoff, almost inaudibly.

"It's no use! Well, let me relate to you how the matter took place. On Saturday evening you were sitting in Klausoff's sleeping room, and drinking vodka and beer with him." (Dukovski fixed his eyes on Psyekoff's face, and kept them there all through the examination.) "Nicholas was waiting on you. At one o'clock, Marcus Ivanovitch announced his intention of going to bed. He always went to bed at one o'clock. When he was taking off his boots, and was giving you directions about details of management, you and Nicholas, at a given signal, seized your drunken master and threw him on the bed. One of you sat on his legs, the other on his head. Then a third person came in from the passage — a woman in a black dress, whom you know well, and who had previously arranged with you as to her share in your criminal deed. She seized a pillow and began to smother him. While the struggle was going on the candle went out. The woman took a box of safety matches from her pocket, and lit the candle. Was it not so? I see by your face that I am speaking the truth. But to go on. After you had smothered him, and saw that he had ceased breathing, you and Nicholas pulled him out through the window and laid him down near the burdock. Fearing that he might come round again, you struck him with something sharp. Then you carried him away, and laid him down under a lilac bush for a short time. After resting awhile and considering, you carried him across the fence. Then you entered the road. After that comes the dam. Near the dam, a peasant frightened you. Well, what is the matter with you?"

"I am suffocating!" replied Psyekoff. "Very well — have it so. Only let me go out, please!"

They led Psyekoff away.

"At last! He has confessed!" cried Chubikoff, stretching himself luxuriously. "He has betrayed himself! And didn't I get round him cleverly! Regularly caught him napping — "

"And he doesn't deny the woman in the black dress!" exulted Dukovski. "But all the same, that safety match is tormenting me frightfully. I can't stand it any longer. Good-bye! I am off!"

Dukovski put on his cap and drove off. Chubikoff began to examine Aquilina. Aquilina declared that she knew nothing whatever about it.

At six that evening Dukovski returned. He was more agitated than he had ever been before. His hands trembled so that he could not even unbutton his greatcoat. His cheeks glowed. It was clear that he did not come empty-handed.

"*Veni, vidi, vici!*" he cried, rushing into Chubikoff's room, and falling into an armchair. "I swear to you on my honour, I begin to believe that I am a genius! Listen, devil take us all! It is funny, and it is sad. We have caught three already — isn't that so? Well, I have found the fourth, and a woman at that. You will never believe who it is! But listen. I went to Klausoff's village, and began to make a spiral round it. I visited all the little shops, public houses, dram shops on the road, everywhere asking for safety matches. Everywhere they said they hadn't any. I made a wide round. Twenty times I lost faith, and twenty times I got it back again. I knocked about the whole day, and only an hour ago I got on the track. Three versts from here. They gave me a packet of ten boxes. One box was missing. Immediately: 'Who bought the other box?' 'Such-a-one! She was pleased with them!' Old man! Nicholas Yermolaïyevitch! See what a fellow who was expelled from the seminary and who has read Gaboriau can do! From to-day on I begin to respect myself! Oof! Well, come!"

"Come where?"

"To her, to number four! We must hurry, otherwise — otherwise I'll burst with impatience! Do you know who she is? You'll never guess! Olga Petrovna, Marcus Ivanovitch's wife — his own wife — that's who it is! She is the person who bought the matchbox!"

"You — you — you are out of your mind!"

"It's quite simple! To begin with, she smokes. Secondly, she was head and ears in love with Klausoff, even after he refused to live in the same house with her, because she was always scolding his head off. Why, they say she used to beat him because she loved him so much. And then he positively refused to stay in the same house. Love turned sour. 'Hell hath no fury like a woman scorned.' But come along! Quick, or it will be dark. Come!"

"I am not yet sufficiently crazy to go and disturb a respectable honourable woman in the middle of the night for a crazy boy!"

"Respectable, honourable! Do honourable women murder their husbands? After that you are a rag, and not an examining magistrate! I never ventured to call you names before, but now you compel me to. Rag! Dressing-gown! — Dear Nicholas Yermolaïyevitch, do come, I beg of you — !"

The magistrate made a deprecating motion with his hand.

"I beg of you! I ask, not for myself, but in the interests of justice. I beg you! I implore you! Do what I ask you to, just this once!"

Dukovski went down on his knees.

"Nicholas Yermolaïyevitch! Be kind! Call me a blackguard, a ne'er-do-weel, if I am mistaken about this woman. You see what an affair it is. What a case it is. A romance! A woman murdering her own husband for love! The fame of it will go all over Russia. They will make you investigator in all important cases. Understand, O foolish old man!"

The magistrate frowned, and undecidedly stretched his hand toward his cap.

"Oh, the devil take you!" he said. "Let us go!"

It was dark when the magistrate's carriage rolled up to the porch of the old country house in which Olga Petrovna had taken refuge with her brother.

"What pigs we are," said Chubikoff, taking

hold of the bell, "to disturb a poor woman like this!"

"It's all right! It's all right! Don't get frightened! We can say that we have broken a spring."

Chubikoff and Dukovski were met at the threshold by a tall buxom woman of three and twenty, with pitch-black brows and juicy red lips. It was Olga Petrovna herself, apparently not the least distressed by the recent tragedy.

"Oh, what a pleasant surprise!" she said, smiling broadly. "You are just in time for supper. Kuzma Petrovitch is not at home. He is visiting the priest, and has stayed late. But we'll get on without him! Be seated. You have come from the examination?"

"Yes. We broke a spring, you know," began Chubikoff, entering the sitting room and sinking into an armchair.

"Take her unawares — at once!" whispered Dukovski; "take her unawares!"

"A spring — hum — yes — so we came in."

"Take her unawares, I tell you! She will guess what the matter is if you drag things out like that."

"Well, do it yourself as you want. But let me get out of it," muttered Chubikoff, rising and going to the window.

"Yes, a spring," began Dukovski, going close to Olga Petrovna and wrinkling his long nose. "We did not drive over here — to take supper with you or — to see Kuzma Petrovitch. We came here to ask you, respected madam, where Marcus Ivanovitch is, whom you murdered!"

"What? Marcus Ivanovitch murdered?" stammered Olga Petrovna, and her broad face suddenly and instantaneously flushed bright scarlet. "I don't — understand!"

"I ask you in the name of the law! Where is Klausoff? We know all!"

"Who told you?" Olga Petrovna asked in a low voice, unable to endure Dukovski's glance.

"Be so good as to show us where he is!"

"But how did you find out? Who told you?"

"We know all! I demand it in the name of the law!"

The examining magistrate, emboldened by her confusion, came forward and said:

"Show us, and we will go away. Otherwise, we — "

"What do you want with him?"

"Madam, what is the use of these questions? We ask you to show us! You tremble, you are agitated. Yes, he has been murdered, and, if you must have it, murdered by you! Your accomplices have betrayed you!"

Olga Petrovna grew pale.

"Come!" she said in a low voice, wringing her hands.

"I have him — hid — in the bath house! Only for heaven's sake, do not tell Kuzma Petrovitch. I beg and implore you! He will never forgive me!"

Olga Petrovna took down a big key from the wall, and led her guests through the kitchen and passage to the courtyard. The courtyard was in darkness. Fine rain was falling. Olga Petrovna walked in advance of them. Chubikoff and Dukovski strode behind her through the long grass, as the odour of wild hemp and dishwater splashing under their feet reached them. The courtyard was wide. Soon the dishwater ceased, and they felt freshly broken earth under their feet. In the darkness appeared the shadowy outlines of trees, and among the trees a little house with a crooked chimney.

"That is the bath house," said Olga Petrovna. "But I implore you, do not tell my brother! If you do, I'll never hear the end of it!"

Going up to the bath house, Chubikoff and Dukovski saw a huge padlock on the door.

"Get your candle and matches ready," whispered the examining magistrate to his deputy.

Olga Petrovna unfastened the padlock, and let her guests into the bath house. Dukovski struck a match and lit up the anteroom. In the middle of the anteroom stood a table. On the table, beside a sturdy little samovar, stood a soup tureen with cold cabbage soup and a plate with the remnants of some sauce.

"Forward!"

They went into the next room, where the bath was. There was a table there also. On the table was a dish with some ham, a bottle of vodka, plates, knives, forks.

"But where is it — where is the murdered man?" asked the examining magistrate.

"On the top tier," whispered Olga Petrovna, still pale and trembling.

Dukovski took the candle in his hand and climbed up to the top tier of the sweating frame. There he saw a long human body lying motionless on a large feather bed. A slight snore came from the body.

"You are making fun of us, devil take it!" cried Dukovski. "That is not the murdered man! Some live fool is lying here. Here, whoever you are, the devil take you!"

The body drew in a quick breath and stirred. Dukovski stuck his elbow into it. It raised a hand, stretched itself, and lifted its head.

"Who is sneaking in here?" asked a hoarse, heavy bass. "What do you want?"

Dukovski raised the candle to the face of the unknown, and cried out. In the red nose, dishevelled, unkempt hair, the pitch-black moustache, one of which was jauntily twisted and pointed insolently toward the ceiling, he recognized the gallant cavalryman Klausoff.

"You — Marcus — Ivanovitch? Is it possible?"

The examining magistrate glanced sharply up at him, and stood spellbound.

"Yes, it is I. That's you, Dukovski? What the devil do you want here? And who's that other mug down there? Great snakes! It is the examining magistrate! What fate has brought him here?"

Klausoff rushed down and threw his arms round Chubikoff in a cordial embrace. Olga Petrovna slipped through the door.

"How did you come here? Let's have a drink, devil take it! Tra-ta-ti-to-tum — let us drink! But who brought you here? How did you find out that I was here? But it doesn't matter! Let's have a drink!"

Klausoff lit the lamp and poured out three glasses of vodka.

"That is — I don't understand you," said the examining magistrate, running his hands over him. "Is this you or not you!"

"Oh, shut up! You want to preach me a sermon? Don't trouble yourself! Young Dukovski, empty your glass! Friends, let us bring this — What are you looking at? Drink!"

"All the same, I do not understand!" said the examining magistrate, mechanically drinking off the vodka. "What are you here for?"

"Why shouldn't I be here, if I am all right here?"

Klausoff drained his glass and took a bite of ham.

"I am in captivity here, as you see. In solitude, in a cavern, like a ghost or a bogey. Drink! She carried me off and locked me up, and — well, I am living here, in the deserted bath house, like a hermit. I am fed. Next week I think I'll try to get out. I'm tired of it here!"

"Incomprehensible!" said Dukovski.

"What is incomprehensible about it?"

"Incomprehensible! For Heaven's sake, how did your boot get into the garden?"

"What boot?"

"We found one boot in the sleeping room and the other in the garden."

"And what do you want to know that for? It's none of your business! Why don't you drink, devil take you? If you wakened me, then drink with me! It is an interesting tale, brother, that of the boot! I didn't want to go with Olga. I don't like to be bossed. She came under the window and began to abuse me. She always was a termagant. You know what women are like, all of them. I was a bit drunk, so I took a boot and heaved it at her. Ha-ha-ha! Teach her not to scold another time! But it didn't! Not a bit of it! She climbed in at the window, lit the lamp, and began to hammer poor tipsy me. She thrashed me, dragged me over here, and locked me in. She feeds me now — on love, vodka, and ham! But where are you off to, Chubikoff? Where are you going?"

The examining magistrate swore, and left the bath house. Dukovski followed him, crestfallen. They silently took their seats in the carriage and drove off. The road never seemed to them so long and disagreeable as it did that time. Both remained silent. Chubikoff trembled with rage all the way. Dukovski hid his nose in the collar of his overcoat, as if he was afraid that the darkness and the drizzling rain might read the shame in his face.

When they reached home, the examining magistrate found Dr. Tyutyeff awaiting him. The doctor was sitting at the table, and, sighing deeply, was turning over the pages of the *Neva*.

"Such goings on there are in the world!" he said, meeting the examining magistrate with a sad smile. "Austria is at it again! And Gladstone also to some extent — "

Chubikoff threw his cap under the table, and shook himself.

"Devils' skeletons! Don't plague me! A thousand times I have told you not to bother me with your politics! This is no question of politics! And you," said Chubikoff, turning to Dukovski and shaking his fist, "I won't forget this in a thousand years!"

"But the safety match? How could I know?"

"Choke yourself with your safety match! Get out of my way! Don't make me mad, or the devil only knows what I'll do to you! Don't let me see a trace of you!"

Dukovski sighed, took his hat, and went out.

"I'll go and get drunk," he decided, going through the door, and gloomily wending his way to the public house.

VIII. Some Scotland Yard Stories — Sir Robert Anderson

When I took charge of the Criminal Investigation Department I was no novice in matters relating to criminals and crime. In addition to experience gained at the Bar and on the Prison Commission, secret-service work had kept me in close touch with "Scotland Yard" for twenty years, and during all that time I had the confidence, not only of the chiefs, but of the principal officers of the detective force. I thus entered on my duties with very exceptional advantages.

I was not a little surprised, therefore, to find occasion to suspect that one of my principal subordinates was trying to impose on me as though I were an ignoramus. For when any important crime of a certain kind occurred, and I set myself to investigate it *à la* Sherlock Holmes, he used to listen to me in the way that so many people listen to sermons in church; and when I was done he would stolidly announce that the crime was the work of A, B, C, or D, naming some of his stock heroes. Though a keen and shrewd police officer, the man was unimaginative, and I thus accounted for the fact that his list was always brief, and that the same names came up repeatedly. It was "Old Carr," or "Wirth," or "Sausage," or "Shrimps," or "Quiet Joe," or "Red Bob," etc., etc., one name or another being put forward according to the kind of crime I was investigating.

It was easy to test my prosaic subordinate's statements by methods with which I was familiar in secret-service work; and I soon found that he was generally right. Great crimes are the work of great criminals, and great criminals are very few. And by "great crimes" I mean, not crimes that loom large in the public view because of their moral heinousness, but crimes that are the work of skilled and resourceful criminals. The problem in such cases is not to find the offender in a population of many millions, but to pick him out from among a few definitely known "specialists" in the particular sort of crime under investigation.

A volume might be filled with cases to illustrate my meaning; but a very few must here suffice. It fell upon a day, for example, that a "ladder larceny" was committed at a country house in Cheshire. It was the usual story. While the family were at dinner, the house was entered by means of a ladder placed against a bedroom window, all outer doors and ground-floor windows having been fastened from outside by screws or wire or rope; and wires were stretched across the lawn to baffle pursuit in case the thieves were discovered. The next day the Chief Constable of the county called on me; for, as he said, such a crime was beyond the capacity of provincial practitioners, and he expected us to find the delinquents among our pets at Scotland Yard. He gave me a vague description of two strangers who had been seen near the house the day before, and in return I gave him three photographs. Two of these were promptly identified as the men who had come under observation. Arrest and conviction followed, and the criminals received "a punishment suited to their sin." One of them was "Quiet Joe"; the other, his special "pal."

Their sentences expired about the time of my retirement from office, and thus my official acquaintance with them came to an end. But in the newspaper reports of a similar case the year after I left office, I recognized my old friends. Rascals of this type are worth watching, and the police had noticed that they were meeting at the Lambeth Free Library, where their special study was provincial directories and books of reference. They were tracked to a bookshop where they bought a map of Bristol, and to other shops where they procured the plant for a "ladder larceny." They then booked for Bristol and there took observations of the suburban house they had fixed upon. At this stage the local detectives, to whom of course the metropolitan officers were bound to give the case, declared themselves and seized the criminals; and the case was disposed of by a nine months' sentence on a minor issue.

Most people can be wise after the event, but even that sort of belated wisdom seems lacking to the legislature and the law. If on the occasion of their previous conviction, these men had been asked what they would do on the termination of their sentence, they would have answered, "Why, go back to business, of course; what else?" And at Bristol they would have replied with equal frankness. On that occasion they openly expressed their gratification that the officers did not wait to "catch them fair on the job, as another long stretch would about finish them" — a playful allusion to the fact that, as they were both in their seventh decade, another penal servitude sentence would have seen the end of them; whereas their return to the practice of their calling was only deferred for a few months. Meanwhile they would live without expense, and a paternal government would take care that the money found in their pockets on their arrest would be restored to them on their release, to enable them to buy more jimmies and wire and screws, so that no time would be lost in getting to work. Such is our "punishment-of-crime" system!

"Quiet Joe" made a good income by the practice of his profession; but he was a thriftless fellow who spent his earnings freely, and never paid income tax. "Old Carr" was of a different type. The man never did an honest day's work in his life. He was a thief, a financier and trainer of thieves, and a notorious receiver of stolen property. But though his wealth was ill-gotten, he knew how to hoard it. Upon his last conviction I was appointed statutory "administrator" of his estate. I soon discovered that he owned a good deal of valuable house property. But this I declined to deal with, and took charge only of his portable securities for money. The value of this part of his estate may be estimated by the fact that on his discharge he brought an action against me for mal-administration of it, claiming £5000 damages, and submitting detailed accounts in support of his claim. Mr. Augustine Birrell was my leading counsel in the suit; and I may add that though the old rascal carried his case to the Court of Appeal he did not get his £5000.

The man lived in crime and by crime; and old though he was (he was born in 1828), and "rolling in wealth," he at once "resumed the practice of his profession." He was arrested abroad this year during a trip taken to dispose of some stolen notes, the proceeds of a Liverpool crime, and his evil life came to an end in a foreign prison.

When I refused to deal with Carr's house property I allowed him to nominate a friend to take charge of it, and he nominated a brother professional, a man of the same kidney as himself, known in police circles as "Sausage." A couple of years later, however, I learned from the tenants that the agent had disappeared, and that their cheques for rent had been returned to them. I knew what that meant, and at once instituted inquiries to find the man, first in the metropolis and then throughout the provinces; but my inquiries were fruitless. I learned, however, that, when last at Scotland Yard, the man had said with emphasis that "he would never again do anything at home." This was in answer to a warning and an appeal; a warning that he would get no mercy if again brought to justice, and an appeal to change his ways, as he had made his pile and could afford to live in luxurious idleness. With this clue to guide me, I soon learned that the man's insatiable zest for crime had led him to cross the Channel in hope of finding a safer sphere of work, and that he was serving a sentence in a French prison.

No words, surely, can be needed to point the moral of cases such as these. The criminals who keep society in a state of siege are as strong as they are clever. If the risk of a few years' penal servitude on conviction gave place to the certainty of final loss of liberty, these professionals would put up with the tedium of an honest life. Lombroso theories have no application to such men. Benson, of the famous "Benson and Kerr frauds," was the son of an English clergyman. He was a man of real ability, of rare charms of manner and address, and an accomplished linguist. Upon the occasion of one of Madame Patti's visits to America he ingratiated himself with the customs officers at New York, and thus got on board the liner before the arrival of the "Reception Committee." He was of course a stranger to the great singer, but she was naturally charmed by his appearance and bearing, and the perfection of his Italian, and she had no reason to doubt that he had been commissioned for the part he played so acceptably. And when the Reception Committee arrived they assumed that he was a friend of Madame Patti's. Upon his arm it was, therefore, that she leaned when disembarking. All this was done with a view to carry out a huge fraud, the detection of which eventually brought him to ruin. The man was capable of filling any position; but the life of adventure and ease which a criminal career provided had a fascination for him.

Facts like these failed to convince Dr. Max Nordau when he called upon me years ago. At his last visit I put his "type" theory to a test. I had two photographs so covered that nothing showed but the face, and telling him that the one was an eminent public man and the other a notorious criminal, I challenged him to say which was the "type." He shirked my challenge. For as a matter of fact the criminal's face looked more benevolent than the other, and it was certainly as "strong." The one was Raymond *alias* Wirth — the most eminent of the criminal fraternity of my time — and the other was Archbishop Temple. Need I add that my story is intended to discredit — not His Grace of Canterbury, but — the Lombroso "type" theory.

Raymond, like Benson, had a respectable parentage. In early manhood he was sentenced to a long term of imprisonment for a big crime committed in New York. But he escaped and came to England. His schemes were Napoleonic. His most famous *coup* was a great diamond robbery. His cupidity was excited by the accounts of the Kimberley mines. He sailed for South Africa, visited the mines, accompanied a convoy of diamonds to the coast, and investigated the whole problem on the spot. Dick Turpin would have recruited a body of bushrangers and seized one of the convoys. But the methods of the sportsmanlike criminal of our day are very different. The arrival of the diamonds at the coast was timed to catch the mail steamer for England; and if a convoy were accidentally delayed *en route*, the treasure had to lie in the post office till the next mail left. Raymond's plan of campaign was soon settled. He was a man who could make his way in any company, and he had no difficulty in obtaining wax impressions of the postmaster's keys. The postmaster, indeed, was one of a group of admiring friends whom he entertained at dinner the evening before he sailed for England.

Some months later he returned to South Africa under a clever disguise and an assumed name, and made his way up country to a place at which the diamond convoys had to cross a river ferry on their way to the coast. Unshipping the chain of the ferry, he let the boat drift down stream, and the next convoy missed the mail steamer. £90,000 worth of diamonds had to be deposited in the strong room of the post office; and those diamonds ultimately reached England in Raymond's possession. He afterward boasted that he sold them to their lawful owners in Hatton Garden.

If I had ever possessed £90,000 worth of anything, the government would have had to find someone else to look after Fenians and burglars. But Raymond loved his work for its own sake; and though he lived in luxury and style, he kept to it to the last, organizing and financing many an important crime.

A friend of mine who has a large medical practice in one of the London suburbs told me once of an extraordinary patient of his. The man was a *Dives* and lived sumptuously, but he was extremely hypochondriacal. Every now and then an urgent summons would bring the doctor to the house, to find the patient in bed, though with nothing whatever the matter with him. But the man always insisted on having a prescription, which was promptly sent to the chemist. My friend's last summons had been exceptionally urgent; and on his entering the room with unusual abruptness, the man sprang up in bed and covered him with a revolver! I might have relieved his curiosity by explaining that this eccentric patient was a prince among criminals. Raymond knew that his movements were matter of interest to the police; and if he had reason to fear that he had been seen in dangerous company, he bolted home and "shammed sick." And the doctor's evidence, confirmed by the chemist's books, would prove that he was ill in bed till after the hour at which the police supposed they had seen him miles away.

Raymond it was who stole the famous Gainsborough picture for which Mr. Agnew had recently paid the record price of £10,000. I may here say that the owner acted very well in this matter. Though the picture was offered him more than once on tempting terms he refused to treat for it, save with the sanction of the police. And it was not until I intimated to him that he might deal with the thieves that he took steps for its recovery.

The story of another crime will explain my action in this case. The Channel gang of thieves mentioned on a previous page sometimes went for larger game than purses and pocket-books. They occasionally robbed the treasure chest of the mail steamer when a parcel of valuable securities was passing from London to Paris. Tidings reached me that they were planning a *coup* of this kind upon a certain night, and I ascertained by inquiry that a city insurance company meant to send a large consignment of bonds to Paris on the night in question. How the thieves got the information is a mystery; their organization must have been admirable. But Scotland Yard was a match for them. I sent officers to Dover and Calais to deal with the case, and the men were arrested on landing at Calais. But they were taken empty-handed. A capricious order of the railway company's marine superintendent at Dover had changed the steamer that night an hour before the time of sailing; and while upon the thieves was found a key for the treasure chest of the advertised boat, they had none for the boat in which they had actually crossed. But, *mirabile dictu*, during the passage they had managed to get a wax impression of it! We also got hold of a cloak-room ticket for a portmanteau which was found to contain some £2000 worth of coupons stolen by the gang on a former trip. The men included in the "bag" were "Shrimps," "Red Bob," and an old sinner named Powell. But the criminal law is skilfully framed in the interest of criminals, and it was impossible to make a case against them. I succeeded, however, by dint of urgent appeals to the French authorities, in having them kept in gaol for three months.

And now for the point of my story. Powell had left a blank cheque with his "wife," to be used in case he came to grief; and on his return to England he found she had been false to him. She had drawn out all his money, and gone off with another man; and the poor old rascal died of want in the streets of Southampton. [1] He it was who was Raymond's accomplice in stealing Mr. Agnew's picture, and with his death all hope of a prosecution came to an end.

If my purpose here were to amuse, I might fill many a page with narratives of this kind. But my object is to expose the error and folly of our present system of dealing with crime. When a criminal court claims to anticipate the judgment of the Great Assize in the case of a hooligan convicted of some vulgar act of violence, the silliness and profanity of the claim may pass unnoticed. But when the "punishment-of-crime" system is applied to criminals of the type here described, the imbecility of it must be apparent to all. With such men crime is "the business of their lives." They delight in it. Their zest for it never flags, even in old age. What leads men like Raymond or Carr to risk a sentence of penal servitude is not a sense of want — that is a forgotten memory. Nor is it even a craving for filthy lucre. The controlling impulse is *a love of sport*, for every great criminal is a thorough sportsman. And in the case of a man who is free from the weakness of having a conscience, it is not easy to estimate the fascination of a life of crime. Fancy the long-sustained excitement of planning and executing crimes like Raymond's. In comparison with such sport, hunting wild game is work for savages; salmon-fishing and grouse-shooting, for lunatics and idiots!

The theft of the Gold Cup at Ascot illustrates what I am saying here. The thieves arrived in motor cars; they were, we are told, "of gentlemanly appearance, and immaculately dressed," and they paid their way into the grand stand. The list of criminals of that type is a short one; and no one need suppose that such men would risk penal servitude for the paltry sum the cup would fetch. A crime involving far less risk would bring them ten times as much booty. For no winner of the cup ever derived more pleasure from the possession of it than the thieves must have experienced as they drove to London with the treasure under the seat of their motor car.

For it was not the lust of filthy lucre, but the love of sport that incited them to the venture. There are hundreds of our undergraduates who would eagerly emulate the feat, were they not deterred by its dangers. And a rule of three sum may explain my proposal to put an end to such crimes. Let the consequences to the professional criminal be made equal to what imprisonment would mean to a "Varsity" man, and the thing is done.

*****

[1] "Shrimps" also found that his "wife" had proved unfaithful. He disappeared, and I heard that he had filled his pockets with stones and thrown himself into the sea. Had the men been in an English gaol they would have communicated with their friends; but in Boulogne prison they were absolutely buried, and their women gave them up.

*****

THE END